'Please don't get the wrong idea!'

Francine spoke rapidly. 'There's been a mistake——'

'Of course,' Alessandro interrupted smoothly. 'You didn't intend to come to my room. And you certainly didn't intend to fall asleep on my bed.'

'No, I *didn't*!' Oh God, what a mess! she thought a little frantically.

His voice became low again. 'There's no need to bother with this little charade, *cara*. I'm not annoyed—on the contrary, it's been a delightful surprise.'

Dear Reader

Whatever the weather this summer, come with us to four places in the sun. In this collection, we offer you the romance you love—with the Latin lovers of the Mediterranean... the colourful sights and sounds of Spain... the excitement and glamour of Venice...the natural beauty of Greece... the relaxed, timeless magic of France. A wonderful tour of sensual delight, with four happy endings along the way! Something sultry from Mills & Boon...

The Editor

Joanna Mansell hasn't always wanted to write. It was an idea that popped into her head when she was 'thirtysomething', and then wouldn't go away again. It's turned out to be rather addictive, though, and now she has started, she says, she can't stop! When she's not working, she loves reading, gardening, watching films, day-dreaming, and sneaking away from the typewriter on hot, sunny days to go for walks along the sea-front.

Recent titles by the same author:

A TOUCH OF APHRODITE

A PERFECT SEDUCTION

BY

JOANNA MANSELL

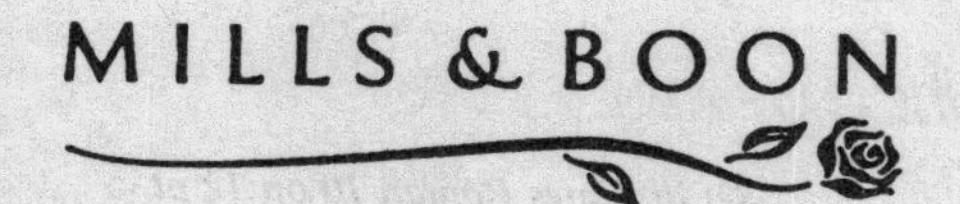

MILLS & BOON LIMITED
ETON HOUSE, 18-24 PARADISE ROAD
RICHMOND, SURREY TW9 1SR

First published in Great Britain 1994
by Mills & Boon Limited

This edition 1994

ISBN 0 263 78519 X

Set in Times Roman 10 on 12 pt.
86-9407-53211 C

Printed in Great Britain by
BPC Paperbacks Ltd
A member of
The British Printing Company Ltd

CHAPTER ONE

DUSK was falling as the *vaporetto* cruised up the Grand Canal in Venice. The heavy heat of the day still hung over the city, and Francine's bright mane of red-gold hair clung damply to the nape of her neck.

She had pushed her way to the very front of the boat, determined not to miss any of the sights. Excitement leapt in her stomach as the boat passed under the Rialto Bridge, its arches etched darkly against the pale stonework. Lamps glowed softly in the gathering darkness, sending golden reflections dancing over the water, and more light spilled from the windows of the shops, houses and grand palazzos that lined the canal. Long, elegant gondolas glided past, and Francine rather enviously stared at their passengers, on the most romantic boat trip of their lives.

Could she afford a trip on one? she wondered. Then she gave a brisk shake of her head, which sent her hair tumbling back over her shoulders in a cascade of colour.

You're here to work, she reminded herself. And if Pete's on his usual form you won't have a minute of free time!

Francine was a photographer's assistant, and Pete was her boss. They were here in Venice to shoot romantic and glamorous photographs for a prestigious calendar. Pete had flown out earlier in the week, to scout out suitable locations before Francine's arrival. And on this occasion Francine wasn't going to be just his assistant. She was also the model!

Pete was a brilliant photographer, and Francine had a flair for administration and organisation. Together, they made a formidable team, but the last year had been tough; the competition for jobs had become increasingly fierce, and they were balancing on a financial knife-edge. Pete had cut costs to the very bone in an effort to undercut the other photographers bidding for this job, and that had included using Francine as a model, so that he wouldn't have to pay a professional.

Francine was willing to do anything to help their small business survive. She wasn't vain, but she knew that her height and excellent bone-structure made her an ideal model. If she had wanted a career in modelling, she could probably have made it to the very top. She wasn't interested, though; she thoroughly enjoyed the job she had.

The *vaporetto* drew in to the landing stage at San Marco, and she quickly picked up her luggage. She always travelled light, and she had a canvas shoulder-bag which held just a change of clothes, and a small holdall for basic toiletries and make-up. Everything else that they would need for the shoot had already been brought here by Pete, at the beginning of the week. She got off the boat and joined the crowds of people already thronging along the banks of the canal. More tourists were heading in the direction of the Piazza San Marco. Francine smiled wryly. This wasn't a good time of the year to be shooting photographs in Venice! Wherever she and Pete went, they were bound to attract an audience of inquisitive tourists, and she knew that she was going to feel very self-conscious, being in front of the camera for once.

She wandered, rather starry-eyed, past the arches and colonnades of the Doge's Palace, and then went on towards the great Piazza in front of the church of San Marco.

Pete had phoned her last night with instructions on how to reach their hotel. 'I'll come and meet you at the landing stage, if you want me to,' he had offered.

'Of course not,' Francine had said at once. 'I'll be fine.' She prided herself on her independence, and she was confident she could find their hotel without any help.

'Well, if you're sure,' Pete had said, with some relief. 'I've still got to find locations for the last couple of photographs, and I really can't afford to waste any time.'

'I'll see you at the hotel,' Francine had told him. 'Bye, Pete.'

And so here she was, poring over the instructions that she had written down, and trying to make some sense of them now that she was actually here, in Venice. She knew that she had to cross the Piazza San Marco and go down one of the quieter side streets on the other side. She began to walk more quickly, leaving most of the crowds behind as she left the piazza.

Once the noisy bustle had faded away, the city seemed to change character and become more mysterious. Heat still rose up from the pavements that had baked in the sun all day and been pounded by thousands of tourists' feet, but it had become a soft, almost sensual warmth now that the city was cloaked in darkness. The lamps that lit the streets were widely spaced, and cast only small pools of light. Francine paused under one of the lamps to study her instructions again. She had to turn left at the end of this street, but when she had done that, she found herself crossing a small canal, and there had been no mention of a canal in Pete's directions.

Beginning to feel uneasy, she retraced her steps and tried another side road, but that took her into a small, unlit alleyway and, suddenly nervous, she hurried through it, hoping to come out into a main street at the other end. She crossed a small courtyard and then found herself walking along a narrow, deserted lane. There was a glint of water ahead, another canal, and she realised that she was beginning to get hopelessly lost.

Francine's confidence was fast evaporating. For one thing, there wasn't anyone else around. And for another, it was *very* dark now, with only a few lights shining from the windows of the houses around her. She had expected to arrive in daylight, but her flight had been held up, so it had been well into the evening by the time she finally reached Venice. She certainly wished it was daylight right now, with the sun blazing down with comforting brightness!

She bit her lip, wondering what to do. The sensible thing would be to retrace her steps, but these back streets of Venice seemed like a maze, and she was no longer sure which direction she had come from.

Then two men stepped on to the bridge that crossed the small canal just ahead of her. Francine looked at them uncertainly. She needed to ask someone for directions, but to walk up to two strange men in a deserted street might be asking for trouble!

They stopped and lounged under the lamp in the centre of the bridge. Francine glanced round nervously, and decided that she had to take a chance. There was no one else around who could help her. She took a deep breath, then walked up to them and held out her piece of paper.

'Excuse me,' she said politely, hoping that at least one of them could speak English. 'Can you tell me how to get to this hotel?'

One of the men stared at her long and hard, then turned to the other and spoke a couple of sentences low and fast in a language that could have been Italian. There was something about his tone of voice that sent a shiver straight up her spine, and she instinctively took a step back. Then he turned and stared at her bag, and she was suddenly quite sure that he was contemplating robbing her. Or worse! Then the other man laughed unpleasantly and let his gaze rake insolently over her, and she knew that she was in deep trouble.

Francine glanced around a little frantically, searching for someone who would help her. The street behind her was deserted, though, and the men knew it, and they grew bolder, advancing towards her. Her heart pounding very fast and loud, she began to back away. One of the men instantly darted round and placed himself in her path, blocking her retreat.

She wanted to yell for help but her throat had gone completely dry. She managed to open her mouth, but it was like a bad dream, absolutely nothing came out. Do something, *do something*, she shrieked at herself silently. Her legs were frozen with fright, though, she couldn't even try to run.

She couldn't believe this was happening; it was ridiculous, the city was jam-packed with people—there must be *someone* who would help her. The street and the bridge were still deserted, though, and the water of the canal below glimmered darkly, with no boats of any kind in sight.

One of the men began to move towards her. Francine forced herself to glare at him as fiercely as she could, but inside she was quite terrified, she knew that she was no match for two strongly built males.

The other one slid round to the far side so that they were flanking her now, preventing her from running off the bridge in either direction. Francine knew that her shaking legs weren't going to carry her anywhere, but they might have just enough strength left to let her scramble over the low balustrade of the bridge and jump into the black, oily water of the canal below. It was a horrible prospect, but it had to be better than letting these men get their hands on her.

She actually had one foot on the balustrade when she heard a hard, authoritative voice grate out a command in Italian from the far end of the bridge.

She didn't understand what had been said, but the forceful tone of voice spoke for itself. An enormous wave of relief washed over her as she realised that someone had finally come to her rescue.

The two men certainly got the message very quickly. One muttered something angrily in a low undertone to the other. Then they turned and looked at the newcomer, as if assessing their chances, two against one.

Francine also turned to look at him. Her heart gave a funny, hard beat that had absolutely nothing to do with the dangerous situation she was in. And, at the same time, she realised why the two men were hesitating, even though the odds were very much in their favour.

The newcomer was dressed almost entirely in black. Black suit, black shoes, and only a glimmer of white from the crisp shirt at his neck. His hair was as dark as his rather formal and beautifully cut clothes, and a scar slashed across his right cheekbone, intensifying the slightly sinister aura that surrounded him. He was inches taller than the two men he was confronting, but more intimidating than that was the aura of physical powerfulness that radiated from him. His eyes glinted in the light from the lamp on the bridge, but their colour remained a mystery. Francine could clearly see the challenge that shone in them, though, as if he were relishing the prospect of a confrontation.

The two men obviously saw it as well. One growled something to the other; then they began to back away, moving even faster as the stranger began to advance threateningly towards them, until they were actually running.

Francine found herself left in the middle of the bridge, facing the dark stranger. Her gaze was still locked on to him, and her pulses were racing unsteadily. She realised that she was almost as frightened of him as she was of the two men who had originally threatened her. It was an entirely different kind of fear, though, and it was edged with the strangest sense of excitement. All of her nerves seemed to be warning her against this man, and yet a shiver almost of pleasure curled up her spine as he took a step nearer.

He became still again, and just looked at her, his eyes locked on to her face with such intensity that she actually stopped breathing for several long, long seconds.

This is ridiculous! she told herself giddily. Say something. Don't just stand here like an idiot.

She swallowed very hard and finally managed to find her voice.

'Thank you,' she got out shakily. 'You came along just in time. I thought I was in real trouble——' Then she stopped, realising that he probably couldn't understand her. And she only knew half a dozen words of basic Italian.

'You *were* in trouble,' he cut in brusquely, in English. 'What the hell were you doing, wandering around these back alleyways by yourself at night?'

'I was lost.' Her voice was horribly quavery, and the shock and relief of hearing him speak English made her legs suddenly wobble like a jelly. 'I was trying to find my hotel——' Without any warning, her legs gave way completely, and she sat down rather abruptly on the balustrade. 'Sorry,' she mumbled. 'I feel rather odd——'

She felt hard fingers twine through her hair, and then a strong hand pushed her head right down and held it there until the world stopped spinning. Francine took a few deep, steadying breaths, and tried not to shiver as that hand slid lightly over her neck before finally releasing her. Then, slowly and very carefully, she stood up again.

'I'm OK now,' she said. Then she shook her head ruefully. 'I always thought that I'd be able to handle it, if something like that ever happened to me. I just froze, though. And then I went to pieces!'

'No one ever knows how they'll react in a situation until it actually happens to them.' His eyes scanned her pale face again. 'My house is nearby,' he said abruptly. 'I suggest that you come home with me, and let my housekeeper look after you. Then, when you're feeling better, I'll take you to your hotel.'

'I'm all right now,' she tried to assure him, but that quiver was suddenly back in her voice again and she knew that she wasn't all right at all. The whole thing had really shaken her, she had hated feeling so helpless and vulnerable.

He didn't argue with her further. Instead, he simply picked up her bag, hooked his fingers around her arm, pulled her to her feet, and then began to walk off, obviously assuming that she would meekly go with him.

Arrogant as well as masterful! Francine thought wryly. At this particular moment, though, she didn't really mind. It was rather a relief to have someone simply take charge of the situation.

She followed him through a maze of dimly lit, narrow alleyways. Then, rather belatedly, she began to wonder if she were quite mad, following a complete stranger through the dark, deserted back streets of Venice. OK, so he had rescued her from those two men, but that didn't automatically mean he was a knight in shining armour!

She was just wondering if she should turn and make a run for it—only he was still carrying her bags, and anyway, where would she go?—when the alleyway suddenly opened out into a much wider road. Francine gave a small sigh of utter relief when she saw other people walking around. Out of all these tourists, some were bound to speak English. If she got into trouble again, all she would have to do was shout for help, and someone would surely come running.

It didn't look as if it would be necessary, though. Despite his slightly sinister appearance, she was beginning to feel increasingly certain that she had never been in any danger from the man who had rescued her. Any nervousness she felt had more to do with her own reaction to him. In his own dark and intimidating way, he was the most gorgeous man she had ever met!

A couple of minutes later, he opened a small door set into the high wall on their left. Francine found herself standing in a small, enclosed courtyard, lit only by the silver moonlight which showed her the shadowy outline of exotic plants in stone urns, the pale gleam of statues, and the glint of water from a sunken pool in the centre.

They crossed the courtyard and went through a second door, which led into the house itself. Francine could see very little of the exterior, but it certainly looked large! Inside, she found herself in an entrance hallway decorated with unexpected opulence. Her rescuer led her up a flight of stairs with elegantly carved banisters, and Francine shot a couple of puzzled looks at the richly coloured paintings that hung on the walls. This was some house!

At the top of the stairs was a corridor lit with a soft glow from half-hidden wall-lights. Moonlight poured in through the long windows that ran right along one side, and Francine couldn't resist peeking out. She saw water, gondolas, people, and the arch of a bridge in the distance, and realised that she was looking directly down at the Grand Canal. She also realised something else. This wasn't just a house. It was a palazzo! One of the grand old palaces of Venice that lined this stretch of the Canal.

Who *was* this man who had rescued her? She realised that she hadn't even asked his name. In fact, there were a whole load of questions that she should have asked him before she agreed to come here with him. Her brain must have been addled with fright, she realised. But she was beginning to feel very much better now, and she wanted some answers.

She quickly caught up with him, and was about to demand to know where she was—and who *he* was—when the high, heavy door they had just been passing suddenly swung open.

Francine stopped dead and blinked as the most amazing sight confronted her.

A huge state room lay beyond the door, decorated with a mixture of exquisite taste and opulence that few people could have achieved or afforded. It was lit by great banks of candles that cast flickering pools of light, but left the far corners wrapped in mysterious shadow. A great gilded mirror on one wall reflected back the candlelight, and overhead shimmered chandeliers created out of tier after tier of dazzling crystals. And the people who filled the room were as impressive as their setting. Beautiful, elegantly groomed people in exquisite dresses and immaculate evening suits.

One of them, a dark-haired woman with the most perfect face Francine had ever seen, walked towards them through the open doorway.

'Alessandro, where have you been?' she asked in a low, sensual voice. Her face and her clothes were Italian, but her accent was American. 'We've missed you.'

Alessandro, Francine repeated silently to herself, the name echoing inside her head.

'I apologise for my absence. There was an unexpected phone call; I had to leave for half an hour to see someone on a very urgent business matter,' he said to the woman, in his distinctive voice. His own English was perfect, with just an intriguing hint of an accent. 'And on the way back I was just in time to prevent a mugging. Or something worse.'

The woman's gaze slid over Francine's dishevelled state. 'The child obviously needs someone to look after her. Take her to Angelina; she enjoys mothering lost strays.'

Francine drew herself up to her full height. She was twenty-one, hardly a child! And that incident tonight had just been unfortunate. Normally, she was very capable of looking after herself.

'I don't need mothering, thank you!' she said indignantly. 'I'd just like to freshen up, and then I'll go to my hotel.'

'Angelina will take care of everything,' Alessandro said firmly. 'Gisella, would you please look after my guests for a short while? I'll be back as soon as I can.'

The dark-haired woman didn't look at all pleased that Alessandro wasn't immediately returning to the party. She opened her exquisitely shaped mouth, as if to say something, but then suddenly closed it again, as if she had learnt that it wasn't a good idea to argue with Alessandro.

Gisella returned to the glittering state room, and Francine followed Alessandro along more corridors and down another flight of stairs. Then he opened another door and she found herself in a huge and surprisingly modern kitchen. At the far end, a plump older woman was bustling around, supervising a handful of younger girls who had obviously been hired as temporary waitresses for the evening. They wore neat, dark uniforms, and were expertly picking up large trays of temptingly prepared food and whizzing through the door with them.

The older woman turned, saw Alessandro, and gave a huge smile. Then she launched into a flood of Italian.

Francine didn't understand a single word. Alessandro listened patiently, though, and when she had finally finished speaking he then gestured towards Francine and began what was obviously an explanation of what had happened this evening, and why she was here.

Sympathy immediately spread over Angelina's face, and she came over and put her plump arm around Francine's shoulder.

'Don't worry,' she said in English. 'I will take care of you.' Then she turned back to Alessandro. 'Come back in an hour. She will be all right by then.'

Alessandro turned to go, but then swung back again. 'I think that I should know your name,' he said, those intense eyes of his boring into her again. In the bright light of the kitchen, she could finally see their colour. They were green, like her own. Then they flickered and changed, became grey. An instant later, they were green again, but the powerful intensity of his gaze didn't change with the colour, and it so unnerved Francine that she almost forgot her own name.

'Francine,' she managed to get out at last. 'Francine Allen.'

'Francine,' he repeated, and something about the way he said it made every nerve in her body feel deliciously on edge. 'And I am Alessandro Zancani,' he went on. Then he waited for a moment, as if half expecting her to show some sign of recognition.

She had never heard his name before, though. And she had certainly never met him before tonight. If she had, she would definitely have remembered. Alessandro Zancani was a very memorable kind of man!

He left the kitchen, and for the next hour Francine was fussed over and pampered in a way that she never had been before, even as a child. She was given hot, strong tea liberally laced with brandy, then Angelina hustled her along to a sumptuous bathroom nearby and encouraged her to use the luxurious soaps, the incredibly soft towels and the subtly scented perfumes that were kept there for the use of guests. Finally, she sat Francine down on a stool and brushed her hair for her, stroking it with a silver-backed brush until it glistened brilliantly.

'Don't you have work to do in the kitchen?' asked Francine, worried that she was taking Angelina away from her duties.

'Everything is organised,' Angelina said at once. 'Anyway, you are more important than food for all those overfed guests. It was terrible that something like that should happen to you on your first evening in Venice.' She stood back and looked at Francine carefully. 'Yes,' she said with some satisfaction, 'you look much better now. Not so pale and shocked. And such beautiful hair! You should always wear it loose. Even Signor Zancani kept looking at it, and he usually likes dark-haired women.'

'Like Gisella?' asked Francine, without thinking. Then she flushed. 'Sorry, none of my business,' she said apologetically.

Angelina's face darkened. 'Signorina Gisella is a—close friend,' she said, in a tone which clearly indicated what she thought of the beautiful Gisella. Then her own brown eyes suddenly sparkled mischievously, as if a slightly wicked idea had sprung into her head. 'Come,' she said, 'Signor Zancani will be coming back soon. We must go and meet him.'

'I certainly want to thank him again for what he did,' agreed Francine. At the same time, though, she glanced a little anxiously at her watch. It was getting late; she should have arrived at her hotel hours ago. As soon as she had thanked Alessandro, she would have to leave.

They returned to the kitchen just as Alessandro walked in the far door. Francine swallowed hard as she saw him. She had forgotten just how gorgeous he was!

Before she could say anything, Angelina stepped forward. 'Signorina Allen is feeling very much better, now. And looking better,' she added, a little slyly. 'Don't you think?'

Alessandro's gaze seemed to be locked on to her face and the bright mane of her hair. With an effort, he tore it away. 'Yes, she looks much better,' he said in an unexpectedly taut voice.

'Her first introduction to Venice was not at all pleasant,' Angelina went on. 'Why not make up for it by inviting her to your party?'

Francine's eyes shot wide open. 'No,' she said at once. 'I can't possibly go to a party.'

'Why not?' said Alessandro, to her surprise.

'I'm—well, I'm—I'm expected at the hotel,' she floundered. 'And, anyway, I don't *know* anyone here.'

'You know me,' Alessandro said softly. 'And there won't be any problem with your hotel. I'll telephone and let them know you've been delayed.'

Francine was alarmed to find herself weakening. She also knew that, hard though she was trying to fight it, she was increasingly fascinated by this man. Her instincts warned her that he was dangerous, but that perversely only made him more interesting.

'I've come to Venice to work, not have fun,' she argued, although without very much conviction.

'It's possible to do both.' His voice was silken, now, and something about the dark undertone set up a small inner trembling deep in Francine's nervous system.

'Go to the party,' Angelina encouraged her. 'Enjoy yourself for a couple of hours. It will help you to forget what happened earlier.'

'I really shouldn't,' Francine said, but the truth was that she was longing to say yes. Her eyes were bright with excitement at the thought of joining the exquisitely dressed people gathered in the state room of this magnificent palazzo. Then her face fell. 'I don't have anything to wear,' she said mournfully. 'I can't go to a party dressed like this!'

She looked down at her crumpled skirt and cotton shirt, and her eyebrows drew together wryly as she compared her travel-creased outfit with the designer dresses she had glimpsed in that state room.

'That can be taken care of,' Alessandro said smoothly. 'Come with me.'

'Have a good time,' Angelina urged, a broad smile on her homely, friendly face.

She's matchmaking! Francine suddenly realised in utter amazement. She's deliberately trying to keep me and Alessandro together for the rest of the evening!

She nearly laughed out loud. The idea that Alessandro could ever be interested in her was just too ludicrous. Epecially when he had someone like the angel-faced Gisella waiting for him in that magnificent state room. And probably in his bed tonight.

That last thought made her unexpectedly wince. Come on, now, she warned herself, with sudden seriousness. Don't start getting involved in anything. You've been given the chance to join in Venetian high society for the evening. Just enjoy it, and don't start dreaming about the impossible.

'I need to phone my hotel before I do anything else,' she said, turning to Alessandro.

'You can use the phone in my study,' he told her. 'I'll show you where it is.'

Francine was quite sorry to leave behind the bright, bustling kitchen, and Alessandro's friendly housekeeper. The rest of the palazzo was slightly overwhelming, with its rich, luxurious furnishings, priceless paintings, silk and velvet covers and curtains, and Venetian crystal.

His study, when they reached it, was lined with shelves of leather-bound books with intricate gold tooling on the spines. In complete contrast was the sophisticated computer, fax machine, and other electronic equipment which equally dominated the room. A curious mixture of the old and the very modern, Francine thought, intrigued.

The phone was on his desk, and she quickly tapped in the number of her hotel. Then her face fell when the person who answered spoke in quick Italian.

'Er—*non capisco*,' she said. 'Do you speak English?'

From the flood of Italian that followed, it was clear that they didn't.

With a wry smile, she turned to Alessandro. 'We're having a communication problem. Can you help?'

He took the phone from her, and held a brief conversation with the person at the other end. When he replaced the receiver, he turned to Francine with a small frown.

'When you didn't turn up at the hotel this evening, they assumed you wouldn't be coming at all. They've re-let your room for tonight.'

'*What*?' yelped Francine.

'It isn't a problem. There are plenty of empty rooms here. You can stay overnight. I'll tell Angelina to arrange it.'

'No,' she said at once. 'I'll find a room somewhere else.'

'This is the very height of the tourist season,' Alessandro pointed out. 'There probably isn't an empty hotel room in Venice.'

'I'll find one,' she insisted.

'You'll stay here,' he said calmly. 'In the morning, you can go to the hotel, as planned. I've told them to make your room available after breakfast.'

'You should have told them to make it available tonight!'

'It's already occupied. And, anyway, it wasn't necessary.'

'I think it was. I don't *want* to stay here!' Then she flushed deeply. 'I didn't mean to be rude,' she said hurriedly. 'I just meant—well, you've already done so much for me tonight.'

'I'm enjoying it,' he said softly. His grey-green eyes glittered briefly, and Francine's stomach abruptly turned right over.

Just one look, and her nervous system went into a state of collapse! she thought with an entirely pleasurable sense of fright. What on earth would a kiss do? Or a caress?

Be sensible, she warned herself. Don't even think about it, because you're never going to get the chance to find out.

'And now we need to find you something to wear for the party,' Alessandro said thoughtfully, his gaze skimming over her in a way that made her skin break out in a small army of goosebumps.

She followed him as he walked off, his stride elegant and easy. Up another flight of stairs—this palazzo was beginning to seem like a maze to her—and then he led her into a dressing-room, where he opened the door of a vast, ornately carved wardrobe. Francine's eyes became huge as she saw the wickedly expensive clothes hanging inside.

'You should find something here that will fit you,' Alessandro told her.

But warning signals were sounding very loud inside her head, now. What kind of man kept a wardrobe full of clothes, for women that he casually brought back to his palazzo? And what kind of woman would wear those clothes?

Not her! Francine decided at once.

'I'm sorry,' she said in a frozen voice. 'I've changed my mind. I want to leave.'

Alessandro suddenly seemed to realise what she was thinking. He became very still and his mouth set into a hard line.

'Do you think that I make a habit of picking women up off the streets and bringing them back here for the night?'

'It certainly looks like it,' Francine retorted. 'Why else would you have all these clothes? I suppose you like them to dress suitably when they get here!'

His eyes gleamed darkly, warning her that she had gone too far. 'These clothes belong to my sister.'

Francine gulped. 'Your—your sister?' she echoed weakly.

'She's about the same size as you. I'm sure that she won't mind if you borrow a dress for the evening.'

Horrified, she realised that she had made the most dreadful mistake. Oh heavens, what on earth could she say?

'I'm sorry. *Very* sorry,' she mumbled inadequately. At the same time, she felt totally stupid. She had jumped to all the wrong conclusions and really behaved very immaturely. 'I shouldn't have said what I did.'

He gave a very cool nod, in acceptance of her apology. 'If you still want to come to the party, find a dress which suits you. Then come down to the state room. I'll be waiting there for you.'

After he had gone, she stood there indecisively for several minutes. Should she leave right now, before something else went wrong? But the clothes were so very tempting, she found herself running her fingers over them, feeling the sleekness of pure silk, the softness of the finest cotton, the harsher texture of gold embroidery.

'It wouldn't hurt to go to the party for just a couple of hours,' she persuaded herself out loud. 'The next few days are going to be very hard work. Why not relax and enjoy yourself this evening?'

She pulled out a couple of dresses; she was absolutely dying to try some of them on. She wriggled into one that was a fantastic concoction of gold trimmed with a riot of feathers, and then giggled. No, not quite her style! In fact, a lot of the dresses were very flamboyant, and she found herself wondering just what Alessandro's sister was like. Very extrovert, if her wardrobe was anything to go by!

Then Francine's eyes gleamed as she spotted a dress at the very end of the rail. It had a long, full skirt of pale green silk, and a tight-fitting sleeveless bodice covered with delicate, intricate embroidery. She very carefully put it on, and then whistled softly when she turned to look at herself in the full-length mirror.

The dress made her look tall and elegant, and her green eyes sparkled with excitement, several shades deeper than the colour of the dress. She brushed her hair until it cascaded down her back in riot of red gold curls, her lips glistened where she had nervously licked them, and a flush of excitement highlighted the delicate line of her cheekbones.

'Wow!' she said softly.

She found matching shoes among the dozens of pairs scattered over the floor of the wardrobe. Filled with new confidence, she left the room, went back down the stairs, and found her way towards the huge open doors that led into the candlelit state room.

When she reached it, though, she held back nervously. She just didn't have the courage to walk inside.

A few moments later, Alessandro came out and found her still hovering uncertainly just outside the door. His gaze slid over her, taking in the stunning dress, and for just an instant his gaze flickered darkly. Then his expression became unreadable and he courteously held out his arm to her.

'Come and meet my guests,' he invited.

Francine wasn't sure what was making her nerves jangle more, the prospect of meeting this roomful of aristocratic strangers or the warm skin and hard muscles that she could feel beneath the fine material of Alessandro's jacket.

They circled slowly around the huge room, and she was relieved when Alessandro introduced her simply as 'a friend'. No mention of the fact that she had nearly been a victim of street crime a couple of hours ago, when he had rescued her. She tried to remember the names of his guests, but there were simply too many. Several were counts, there were a couple of princes, and quite a few of the faces were recognisable because they were well known through films, the theatre, the arts or top-ranking sports events.

A glass of champagne was pressed into her hand, and she quickly drank it. She was very aware of Alessandro watching her as she slowly moved among his guests. Even when she turned away from him, she could seem to feel that hard gaze locked on to her with disturbing intensity.

The candles flickered and flared, making her feel slightly dizzy. Or was it Alessandro who was making her head spin?

Her heart gave an odd, irregular thump as he walked back to join her.

'People are intrigued by you,' he said softly. 'They want to know who you are, where you come from.'

'They would probably be very disappointed if they knew the truth. I'm really very ordinary,' she said, with a wry smile.

His grey-green gaze fixed on her face until the blood beat hotly under her skin. Then it slid down, lingering on the generous swell of her body beneath the glistening silk, before moving up again to the bright strands of her hair. His hand moved slightly, as if he were tempted to touch them. Francine found that she had almost stopped breathing.

'Would you like some more champagne?' he murmured.

'No, I—I think that I've had quite enough,' she got out breathlessly.

'Of course you haven't,' Alessandro said, the low, velvet tones of his voice like a caress. 'Tonight, there are no limits, no rules, Francine. You're allowed to have anything that you want.' His eyes challenged her silently, the sheer power of his gaze not allowing her to look away from his scarred, arrogant face. 'What *do* you want, Francine?'

'Nothing,' she somehow managed to lie in a choked voice. 'Absolutely nothing.'

Then she finally tore her gaze from his and hurried away, as if he had suddenly turned into the most dangerous man in the world. And perhaps he had, because she had had the terrifying feeling that he had known exactly what she had wanted as his eyes had looked right into her hungry soul.

CHAPTER TWO

FRANCINE quickly gulped down another glass of champagne, even though she hadn't intended to drink any more this evening. She definitely needed something to try and calm her fractured nerves! The champagne only seemed to add to the hot flush of excitement in the pit of her stomach, though.

What on earth was happening to her tonight? she wondered with a mixture of apprehension and a strange sense of anticipation. How could a complete stranger—well *almost* a stranger; she was already beginning to feel as if she had known Alessandro for an incredibly long time—send all her nerve-endings into this giddy confusion?

The orchestra played on, the candles glowed softly, and the beautiful and famous people who filled this magnificent state room laughed and danced, drank and talked. English was the main language, although Francine heard conversations being conducted in French and Italian. She danced a couple of times with men who paid her subtle compliments, drank more champagne, and was aware that Alessandro wasn't the only one watching her with uncomfortable intensity. Gisella was also watching every move that she made. And it was very clear that the older woman didn't like her transformation from bedraggled waif to sophisticated guest!

Francine's legs and feet finally began to tremble a little with sheer weariness. She had been up since dawn, it had been a long day—and one full of surprises—and she had drunk too much champagne.

A clock nearby melodically chimed midnight, and her mouth curved into a faint smile. Like Cinderella, it was time to leave the ball!

She looked round for Alessandro, and saw that he was now standing next to Gisella. Francine gave a small grimace, but her mind was made up. If she stayed here much longer, she was going to fall asleep on her feet!

She walked over to Alessandro and looked at him a little apologetically. 'It's been a lovely party, but I really am very tired.'

'Of course,' he said at once. 'I'll ask Angelina to show you to your room.'

Gisella's dark head immediately came up. 'Her room?' she repeated sharply. 'She's staying here?'

'Just for the one night,' Francine said quickly. She didn't want to cause trouble between Alessandro and this woman.

'She is my guest,' Alessandro said in a very cool tone, and Gisella must have got the message at once because she didn't say anything more. Her beautiful eyes spoke volumes, though, and, if looks could have killed, Francine would have shrivelled up right then and there on the floor!

As Alessandro guided her out of the state room, Francine turned to him a little anxiously. 'Look, if it's going to cause problems for you, I don't have to stay. I'm sure I can find a room somewhere——'

'It's past midnight, and I'm certainly not going to turn you out on to the street at this hour,' he cut in.

'But Gisella——' she began awkwardly.

'Gisella is an old friend.' Alessandro's tone clearly indicated that the conversation was at an end. They walked on in silence, and a minute later Francine was delivered into Angelina's capable hands.

'Did you enjoy the party?' asked his housekeeper, looking first at her, and then at her employer.

'Yes, I did,' said Francine, quite truthfully.

'It's a shame that you couldn't stay longer,' Angelina said with a touch of dispapointment. She obviously didn't want to see Alessandro return alone to the party—and Gisella's clutches.

'Francine is very tired,' Alessandro said, with a severe but not angry look at his housekeeper. He was clearly used to her good-natured meddling in his private life. Then he turned back to Francine. 'The party will probably go on until the small hours of the morning. I hope the noise doesn't disturb you.'

'I'm so tired that I could sleep through anything,' she said frankly. 'And thank you very much for looking after me so well.'

'It's been my pleasure,' he said softly. The look he gave her made her toes curl right up, and she knew that she had gone faintly pink. Then he left, to return to his guests, and she couldn't quite stifle a faint sigh of regret.

'You like him?' said Angelina, with some satisfaction. 'Of course you do,' she went on, answering her own question. 'All the women like him. He never allows himself to be caught by any of them, though,' she added, with a small sigh.

'Not even by Gisella?' Francine couldn't help asking.

Angelina gave a rude snort. 'The day she comes into this house as its mistress, I leave! And Signor Zancani knows that. It's why he'll never propose to her,' she went on with a big grin. 'Wives are easy to find, but good housekeepers are very rare.'

'Gisella looks Italian, but sounds American,' Francine said, for some reason unable to leave the subject alone.

'Her father is American and her mother Italian. She has a home in America, but spends a lot of time in Venice—especially when Signor Zancani is here,' Angelina said meaningfully.

Francine hurriedly decided that she had pried enough into Alessandro's private life. If he came back unexpectedly and heard them talking about him—— She gave a small shiver, and decided that she didn't even want to think about the possible consequences!

'I think I'd better go up to my room,' she said to Angelina. 'Can you show me where it is?'

A few minutes later she had been installed in a small but luxurious bedroom on the first floor. There was an adjoining bathroom with absolutely everything a guest could possibly need, and the bed itself, although old with a massive, carved headboard, looked soft and welcoming.

'If you need anything, just ring,' Angelina instructed, pointing to a tasselled bellrope. 'Sleep well.'

She closed the door behind her as she went out, and Francine suddenly felt very alone. That was ridiculous, she told herself severely. The palazzo was still full of people! She could hear the faint sounds of the party drifting up from below.

Although she was so very tired, she also felt oddly restless. She wandered around the room for a while, feeling as if she shouldn't be here.

Well, you *shouldn't*, she reminded herself. You should be in your hotel, not spending the night in a palazzo!

Francine gave a sudden grin. What would her friends say if they could see her now, about to climb into this great old bed in a room that looked out over the Grand Canal? Would they go green with envy when she told them that she had accepted an invitation from a perfect stranger to the most impressive party she had ever been to, and then spent the evening drinking champagne and dancing with counts and princes?

And her father? How would *he* react when she told him about tonight's little adventure?

Francine's parents had split up when she was very young, and her mother had been given custody of her, but she had always kept in touch with her adored father. He was Paul Allen, but he was far better known to his fans as Paul James, the film star. Francine was very proud of her father's success, although even now, grown up as she was, she was still rather dazzled by his flamboyant and extravagant lifestyle. Her father hated dullness and routine, anything ordinary. When Francine went to visit him, she found herself embroidering details of her own social life, trying to make it sound much more interesting than it really was. Deep down, she had always had a secret fear that he would one day decide that *she* was dull and ordinary, and simply lose interest in her.

Common sense told her that wouldn't happen, that he really loved her, and it didn't matter that her lifestyle couldn't match his own, but that small fear would never quite go away. She even made her job sound much more glamorous when she was telling him about it, giving the impression that they were always shooting off to exotic locations, meeting famous people and working with top models, when in fact that kind of assignment only came up once in a blue moon.

For once, though, she wouldn't have to exaggerate. Tonight had been the real thing, that rescue by a tall, dark stranger who had then whisked her back to his palazzo and turned her into a princess, so that she could go to the ball.

Pure fantasy, Francine told herself with a bemused shake of her head. That was what the entire evening had been. It was no wonder that she couldn't relax! She would take a bath, she decided, and get ready for bed. Perhaps she would feel more like herself when she had taken off the green silk dress and put on her old cotton nightshirt!

At that point, Francine realised that her bags hadn't been brought up to the room. What was she supposed to sleep in? Nothing at all? *Not* a good idea, she told herself sternly. What if there were some kind of emergency, and she had to rush out in the middle of the night?

She reached for the bellrope, intending to ring for Angelina, but then stopped. Alessandro's housekeeper had had a very busy evening; organising a party on that scale must have meant a huge amount of work. Francine didn't want to tire her further, making her run up and down stairs in search of her lost luggage. She would find it herself.

She tried to remember where she had last seen her holdall. Alessandro had been carrying it—and he had left it in the room where she had changed into the green silk dress, she remembered in triumph. There, it was simple! All she had to do was find that room.

Francine opened the bedroom door and slipped out into the darkened corridor outside. She pushed open several doors, beginning to yawn hard now. Where *was* that dressing-room, where she had changed clothes earlier in the evening?

Then she pushed open a door at the very far end of the corridor and found herself standing on the threshold of another bedroom. And what a room it was! Several times the size of her own, and dominated by the most enormous bed with carved pillars at the four corners. Silk sheets shimmered in the silver moonlight that poured through the windows, and overhead hung a spectacular chandelier of what surely had to be Venetian glass.

Francine couldn't resist the temptation to peep further inside. The room was clearly empty, she thought it was probably a guest room that was reserved for *very* special guests.

She tiptoed over to the window and found herself gazing down at the Grand Canal. In the distance, she could see the Rialto Bridge, beautifully illuminated, and even though it was well past midnight, people were still wandering around in the sultry heat of the night. She watched enviously as a gondola glided past silently with a pair of lovers on board, arms twined around each other. Francine gave a soft sigh. The dark, velvet night, the midsummer warmth which had wrapped itself around the city, was making her own body feel hot and restless, despite her tiredness.

She found herself suddenly thinking of Alessandro. An image of his dark, scarred face etched itself on her mind, and at the same time a light shiver ran the entire length of her spine.

Forget about him, she warned herself. She didn't belong in his world, and she wouldn't even see him again after tonight. She would be working hard, helping Pete shoot the photos for the calendar, then she would be going back to England while Alessandro stayed here in Venice—with Gisella.

It was funny—and rather alarming—how much she hated that idea. Hated the thought of them being together.

Don't even think about it, Francine told herself sternly. She forced herself to look out of the window again, at the shadowed splendour of the Grand Canal, and almost succeeded in pushing all thoughts of Alessandro right out of her head. Almost...

She found herself yawning as a fresh wave of tiredness swept over her. She turned away from the window and stared longingly at the bed, which looked so blissfully soft and welcoming. On impulse, she sat on the very edge of it, and it was as marvellously comfortable as she had expected.

The temptation to stretch right out on it was just too great. She told herself it would only be for a few seconds, she just wanted to know what it would feel like to let her tired body sink into that feather soft mattress.

Guiltily, she climbed on to the bed, then she wriggled her toes and gave a small sigh of pure contentment. She certainly hadn't had a deprived childhood, but she had never slept on silk sheets! They felt sensually smooth and cool against her hot skin.

Francine reminded herself that she had to go back to her own room, she had no business being in here. First of all, though, she had to straighten out this bed. She certainly didn't want anyone to know that she had sneaked on to it and tried it out for a couple of minutes.

It was such an effort to move, though. She felt quite irresistibly sleepy, and although she told herself that she mustn't, really *mustn't* do it, she found herself closing her eyes for just a few moments, trying to imagine what it would be like to spend an entire night in this magnificent bed.

A few seconds later, without any warning at all, she slid straight into a deep sleep.

When she finally opened her eyes again, she didn't have the vaguest idea where she was. She seemed to be floating on something so soft that it felt like drifting on a sea of clouds, and her eyes began to droop shut again as she gave in to the overwhelming desire to go straight back to sleep.

Then she heard what must have awakened her in the first place, a small noise, like—like someone moving around the room, she suddenly realised with a nervous gulp.

Instantly, she was completely awake. And, at the same time, everything came rushing back with nerve jarring clarity. She was in the huge, luxurious bedroom at the palazzo. And she was *not* in her own bed.

Her pulses thumping, Francine sat up.

'Is—is someone there?' she asked in a very quavery voice.

'Of course I'm here,' a man's voice answered silkily. It was already a very familiar voice, and Francine's heart felt as if it had just stopped beating. Then she felt the bed move as the weight of Alessandro's body settled on to it. 'How clever of you to find your way to my room,' he went on. There was a faintly cynical note in his voice which she hadn't heard before, and she realised immediately why that cynicism was there. He didn't believe that she was in his room—his bed—by accident!

'Please, don't get the wrong idea,' she said very rapidly. 'There's been a mistake——'

'Of course,' Alessandro interrupted smoothly. 'You didn't intend to come to my room. And you certainly didn't intend to fall asleep on my bed.'

'No, I *didn't*.' Oh, God, what a mess! she thought a little frantically. And what a stupid, *stupid* thing to do, falling asleep like that. And in Alessandro's bed, of all places!

His voice became low again, and its soft cadences almost seemed to stroke her skin as he replied. 'There's no need to bother with this little charade, *cara*. I'm not annoyed at finding you here. To the contrary, it's been a rather delightful surprise.'

Francine was devastated to find herself responding to his words with a hot flush of pleasure that swept over her entire body. This man's voice, the faint masculine scent of his body seemed to be weaving a dark spell over her. She made a rather desperate attempt to shake off his hypnotic influence, and regain some of her usual common sense.

In the pale moonlight, she could see little more than the dark outline of his body as he sat elegantly on the bed beside her. She drew back as far as she could. The more distance she could put between them, the safer she felt!

'I didn't fall asleep on your bed to surprise you,' she said very firmly.

Even in the darkness, she could see the smile that lifted the corners of Alessandro's hard mouth.

'Do you want to pretend that none of this was planned?' he said with obvious amusement. 'Yes, I think I'd like that,' he went on a little more huskily. 'I like to play games.'

But Francine had enough sense left to realise that she would be getting involved in the most dangerous game of her life. It was definitely time to put a stop to this, and leave.

She tried to scramble off the bed, but was stopped by strong fingers which gripped her slender wrist.

It was the first physical contact between them, and for a few moments it drove all the protests out of Francine's head. She felt the blood in her veins throb under his touch; felt her own hand grow first cold with shock, and then very hot.

Alessandro was also very still for a moment, as if caught unexpectedly off guard. Then he gave a low laugh and released her. 'You keep surprising me. No one's done that for a very long time. Perhaps that's why I'm letting you play with me like this.'

'I'm not playing at anything!' she insisted at once.

'Of course you are. So were most people at the palazzo tonight. The evening was meant to be a mixture of fun and intrigue. It was a sophisticated party for some very sophisticated people.'

Before Francine could confess that she really wasn't very sophisticated at all, that if she gave that impression then it was just a façade, Alessandro had run his fingers lightly up the thin, vulnerable inner skin of her wrists. Involuntarily, she shivered. Then he bent his dark head, his lips brushed against hers in the darkness, and this time the shiver that ran through her was absolutely enormous. And not in the least unpleasant.

'Cold?' queried Alessandro, as he sensed her reaction. His hands found hers and lay against them. 'No, not cold,' he went on thoughtfully, as the heat of her palms beat against his own. 'Just aroused.'

'I—I am *not*,' she denied in utter confusion.

'Oh, but you are, *cara*,' he said softly. 'Believe me. I know about these things.'

And she had no trouble at all believing that! At the same time, she realised that her heart had begun to thump so fast that it was making her head whirl, and it wasn't just her palms that were hot. The whole of her body seemed to be burning up, as if she were suddenly feverish.

It was a perfectly normal reaction, she tried to convince herself. Anyone's nervous system would go haywire if they woke up out of a deep sleep and found a man in the room. In fact, sitting on the bed! And *especially* if he were a man like Alessandro.

As well as that, she had drunk far too much champagne at that party. She could still feel it fizzing very pleasantly through her veins and bubbling gently in the pit of her stomach.

Francine quickly decided that the best thing—in fact, the only thing—to do, was to get out of here right now. She was quite certain that this situation could very easily get right out of hand. More alarming than that, she didn't completely trust herself in this hot, effervescent mood. Even now, she could feel herself weakening again as she felt the warmth of Alessandro's skin against her own.

First of all, though, she had to get off this bed. And, as she was only too aware, Alessandro was still holding on to her hand.

She cleared her throat very nervously, and wished that she could see him more clearly. She dearly wanted to see the expression on his face. Perhaps then she would be able to tell if he was taking this seriously, or simply teasing her. His voice gave so little away, the tone sometimes cool, sometimes husky, sometimes amused, but never quite revealing what lay behind the complex façade.

She took a deep breath and then made a determined effort to pull her hand free. Alessandro released her at once, and Francine was alarmed to discover that she immediately missed his firm, hard grip.

Get hold of yourself! she ordered herself silently. You can't have these kind of feelings about someone you've only known for a few hours.

It was already hard to believe that they had met this evening for the first time, though. She felt as if she had known him for so much longer, for something inside her sparked into life whenever he was near. Without even trying, he could make her feel nervous, excited, pleasurably frightened, aroused—yes, aroused, she realised with a small jolt. And that was frightening in an entirely different way.

It was also something of a new experience for Francine. The couple of semi-serious relationshps she had had in her twenty-one years had turned out to be a big disappointment. There had been kisses, which she had quite enjoyed, but when things had finally gone further the rather clumsy fumblings just hadn't touched her at all. She had even begun to be afraid that she might be cold, incapable of the intense desires which other people seemed to experience, and which she had read about, sometimes dreamed about.

But she definitely didn't feel cold tonight! And Alessandro *knew* it. His fingers began to trace their delicate pattern of caresses over the inner skin of her wrists again, and she swallowed hard.

'Can we—can we turn on the light?' she asked in a small voice. Perhaps she would be able to think straight—behave sensibly—if the room weren't so dark.

'No lights,' he told her.

'Why not?'

'Because it's more interesting in the dark.' The huskiness was returning to his own voice, and Francine felt her own throat grow dry. 'To be able to touch and explore, but not to see.'

'I'm frightened of the dark,' she said, and it wasn't altogether a lie. Being in this shadowed room with him was certainly scaring her half to death!

'You're not frightened,' Alessandro said at once, with absolute certainty. 'You're apprehensive—which isn't the same thing at all. And you're intrigued, you want to know more—do more. So do I,' he finished softly.

Francine gulped. It really was quite terrifying that a man who had been a complete stranger just a few hours ago could read her thoughts—her emotions—with such devastating accuracy.

'It's like an adventure, isn't it?' he murmured. 'And I think that you like adventures.'

She tried to tell him that she didn't, she really didn't, but the words just wouldn't come out. Perhaps it was the warm touch of his fingers that was stifling her voice. Or maybe his caressing tone, which did such distracting things to her nervous system. Or—perhaps most frightening of all—he had simply put his finger on the truth.

There *was* a part of her that was more than ready for excitement and new experiences, a break from the rather dull routine that her personal life seemed to have slid into lately. Oh, yes, she made up stories to tell her father of romantic men she had met in exotic places, but the truth was that she and Pete had worked so very hard this year to keep the business afloat that there had been hardly any spare time for a social life of any kind.

But here she was, in the most romantic city in the world with a man whose voice was like velvet; whose hands were still moving lightly up and down her bare arms, silently promising all kinds of unknown pleasures.

It was so very hard to resist; and Francine didn't even want to. She simply wanted to reach out and grasp what he was offering her.

No, no, *no*, she told herself with a small shiver. You can't do it.

Alessandro moved a little closer. The moonlight shone on their bodies, and she could see the pale gleam of her silk dress, the thin folds brushing aginst his much darker clothing; see his deeply tanned hands etched against the whiteness of her own bare arms.

He must have followed her gaze, because he held his hand up against hers, one looking almost white and the other almost black; positive and negative.

'Darkness and light,' he murmured. 'Two complete opposites, but I think that we complement each other.' His hand moved up to her hair, letting the red-gold strands spill over his fingers. 'Everything about you is bright.'

She allowed her fingers to brush lightly against his own hair, feeling an acute sense of pleasure as its crispness curled against her skin. 'Is it dark brown, or black?' she asked him unsteadily. It had been impossible to tell in the softly lit palazzo.

'Black, of course. Like the night. Like my soul.' That last sentence was said in a mocking tone, but Francine still believed him. There was something about Alessandro that *was* dark. Perhaps that was part of his attraction, the element of danger, the knowledge that he could take her to places where she had never dared to set foot before.

She shook her head, told herself to *stop*. And she really had to leave, right now—or she might not go at all!

She sat up very straight, and nervously licked her lips. 'I think that it's time I went back to my own room.'

'If you didn't intend to stay, why come here in the first place?'

'I told you, it was a mistake. I never intended to fall asleep on your bed, and I certainly didn't want you to find me here. I know that you don't believe me, but it happens to be the truth. I'm sorry if you're—disappointed. And I also apologise for trespassing in what is clearly a private room.'

'I'm not disappointed,' Alessandro said softly. 'And whether you meant to be here or not doesn't seem particularly important. I won't throw you out—if you don't want to go.'

'I *do* want to go,' she insisted, but there was an alarming lack of conviction in her voice. How on earth was she going to convince him that she meant what she said, when she couldn't even convince herself?

His eyes gleamed in the darkness, challenging her. 'You want to leave before the adventure has even properly begun?'

'I'm not interested in this kind of adventure.'

'Of course you are. Tonight can be whatever we want it to be,' he said softly, persuasively. 'Fantasy time. Games for lovers. Why not try pretending that I'm your lover, Francine? Your perfect lover.'

Another shiver racked her. Dangerous games—tempting games. What woman could resist the perfect lover?

Alessandro's fingers slid down her spine, following the path of that last deep shiver. Every time he touched her, Francine could feel her self-control slipping a little further away from her. And he knew it, he had to know it. She had the terrifying, fascinating feeling that he knew everything about this side of her nature. While she knew hardly anything at all——

His mouth found hers again in the darkness, and brushed against it with light kisses, tantalising kisses, promising so much more if she only had the courage to take what he was offering. There was none of the slightly clumsy, fumbling lovemaking that she had experienced in the past. Only the light, sure touch of hands that knew exactly what they were doing.

And the choice was hers. He was tempting her, but there was no force, no coercion. Just those devastating caresses that were merely a promise of what was to come, if she stayed. She was free to run away—if she wanted to. Francine certainly knew that she should, but she was becoming completely spellbound by what was happening. What was it he had said? Light and dark complemented each other. And she was beginning to believe him; he made her feel half of a whole.

But he made her feel other things as well. Dark, disturbing sensations began to well up inside her as his kisses became more intense, and his hands explored more intimately. He slid the bright hair from her shoulders, let his mouth explore the soft, warm skin at the nape of her neck, then murmured a velvet invitation in her ear to learn more about him.

Oh, this was a strange night, Francine thought hazily. Or perhaps she was still asleep, and dreaming. Asleep or awake, though, nothing in her entire life had ever been like this before.

She closed her eyes and let the dream take over. She felt his hands slide under the soft silk of her dress, causing her to catch her breath in a tiny gasp. She was beginning to realise that this was escapism on a grand scale, tonight she had the chance to be—and do—whatever she wanted. The entire evening had been one big fantasy, being rescued from danger by a dark stranger, brought to this magnificent palazzo, and then spending the evening dancing by candlelight and drinking champagne.

No wonder she had almost convinced herself that none of it was real. The silk against her skin, the warm darkness of the room, the growing heat of the man lying beside her—it could all so easily be just a figment of her fevered imagination.

Alessandro was kissing her again now, and she was letting him; she knew that she shouldn't, but those intense kisses simply melted away all thoughts of resistance. His voice—already so familiar—murmured in her ear, suggesting quite outrageous things, but she wasn't shocked; instead she found herself hotly *wanting* to do every single one of those things.

The room began to spin around her, she was entranced by the sound of his voice, the touch of his hands. Gently but inexorably, he led her along paths that she had never travelled along before. And every step she took made it that much harder to stop and turn back. The warmth of the room was nothing compared to the burning heat spreading through her body.

She found herself reaching out and touching hot, hard skin; felt the rhythmic but racing beat of a heart that pounded against a strong ribcage; became aware of hidden pulses that beat in time with her own.

In turn, warm lips slid over her breasts, hands teased small storms of pleasure from the aching tips, and Alessandro's dark velvet voice began to talk to her again, quickly becoming more ragged, as if he were being pushed against his will to the very limits of his control.

Briefly, he raised his head. 'So many surprises,' he said huskily. 'I didn't expect——'

'Didn't expect what?' she managed to say dazedly, astounded that she was still capable of saying anything at all that made sense.

But he didn't answer her. Instead, his strong arms pulled her closer. She could smell shared sweat, feel shared heat, and for the first time in her life felt the terrifying and exhilarating tug of shared deep, dark desire.

Francine felt as if she were drowning, melting, but no longer dreaming, no, definitely *not* dreaming, this was the most real thing that had ever happened to her. And she wanted, oh, she wanted——

He knew exactly what she wanted. But he also knew how to control it so that she was always hungry for a little more.

The slide down into pleasure became exquisitely drawn out, and Francine began to give up any hope of ever being able to climb back up into sanity. The silk dress was eased further away from her, she was touched and licked and caressed until her skin felt raw with pleasure. Her breasts, already soft and full, became even more swollen for him as the blood pounded through her veins. Alessandro murmured with satisfaction, then kissed one hot, aching nipple as if to reward her.

A part of her knew that she was being deliberately seduced—and she didn't care. He was making her feel all the things that she had always wanted to feel, but never could. Every touch of his fingers made her skin burn. Her mouth was aching from his kisses, but still longed for more. She lay back as his tongue provoked small explosions of pleasure from her trembling body.

But then his hand slid gently between her thighs and she suddenly stiffened. Despite everything, she hadn't been quite ready for that.

'Don't tense up,' Alessandro said very softly, his voice a persuasive whisper against her ear. 'Relax—just relax——'

But she couldn't do it, even though his gently moving fingers were already sending tiny waves of a new and intense pleasure right through her. Her teeth clamped together and all her muscles went rigid as she instinctively resisted him.

'Why are you fighting me?' His gleaming eyes looked down at her challengingly. 'Moral scruples? But it's a little late for that.'

'I just don't want—I never meant——' she said in a barely coherent voice.

He drew back and she immediately missed his touch, his warmth, his powerful, confident body.

'I play games, but not this kind of game,' he warned in a voice that suddenly had a hardened edge to it. 'Make a decision right now. Run away or stay.' His eyes bored into her again, hot and glittering. 'What are you going to do, Francine?'

CHAPTER THREE

FRANCINE ran. She clutched the silk dress to her half-naked body and rushed back to the safety of her room, slamming the door shut behind her.

'Coward, *coward*,' she berated herself. But, when it came down to it, even in a fantasy she couldn't turn herself into someone she wasn't.

Her father thought she was a free spirit, changing partners as easily as she changed clothes. That was the impression she had deliberately given him, wanting him to believe that her lifestyle was as carefree and irresponsible as his own. The real Francine, though, despite her dazzling looks, was just a little old-fashioned.

And now you've blown your chance to spend the night with a man who could have convinced you, once and forever, that you're not cold in bed, she told herself with a deep sigh. The kind of man you'll probably never meet again in your entire lifetime.

Too late now, though, for regrets. She had made her decision, and would just have to live with it.

She carefully hung up the green silk dress and knew that she would never wear anything quite like it again. Not unless she married a millionaire! Then she stepped into the shower and let the cool water run for a long time over her still hot and aching body.

Finally in bed, it was so hard to sleep. She couldn't forget Alessandro's kisses, or the silk-soft touch of his hands. She could still seem to smell his crisp, masculine scent and she *knew* that if she closed her eyes she would only see his face.

Francine stared into the darkness and wished that she had never come to Venice. Just one night here, and her life seemed to have turned topsy-turvy. She realised that she wanted——

It's no use wanting what you can never have, she told herself with fresh determination. She shut her eyes, ordering herself to go to sleep. But there was still that funny ache inside her, and she *could* see every detail of Alessandro's dark, scarred face behind her closed eyelids.

She at last managed a couple of hours of restless sleep, waking up again just after dawn. Another hot, perfect day was dawning over Venice, and she gave a small sigh. It was time to return to reality. Time to go.

She silently opened the door to her bedroom and found her bag standing just outside. Someone must have put it there very late last night. Quickly, she pulled out some of her own clothes and wriggled into them. Then she picked up her bag and crept down the corridor. She wanted to leave now, before anyone else was awake. Before she had to face Alessandro Zancani again!

Francine knew that she wouldn't know what to say. She didn't even know if she could look at him, not after the intimate secrets they had shared last night. It might not have meant much to him, he was too mature and experienced, but it had certainly been a milestone in her life. She had always thought that intense sexual desire would grow out of a loving relationship. She had certainly never expected it to happen with a stranger!

She found a staircase that led down, and followed it, her feet stumbling a little on the steps that had worn unevenly over the centuries. It took her down to the ground floor, where the rooms were darker, damper, and less well furnished than the magnificent rooms on the upper floors. Then she came to a door with heavy bolts. With an effort, she pulled them back, and then pushed the door open.

She found herself facing the Grand Canal. She must have come out through an exit at the back of the palazzo. Heat was already beating down from the rising sun, the bright light bouncing back in dazzling flashes from the water and brilliantly illuminating the palazzos that lined the canal, every detail of their faded splendour standing out in sharp relief. Francine's own skin already felt hot—or had that hot ache from last night *still* not gone?

A water taxi chugged round the bend in the canal. There was a small jetty behind the palazzo, and Francine walked out on to it and hailed that taxi. She bundled herself and her bag on board, then sat and shivered slightly, despite the heat. The boat moved off and she told herself that she wouldn't look back, but her head seemed to turn of its own accord. Then her heart suddenly gave a gigantic thump and almost stopped beating, because a tall, dark figure had appeared on the jetty.

She knew at once that it was Alessandro. He didn't move, though, didn't signal to her in any way. He simply stood there and watched as the boat carried her further away. Then the water taxi began the long curve round to the Ponte dell'Accademia, and the palazzo, and its dark, arrogant owner, were lost from sight.

Francine felt a huge pang of regret. The adventure was finally over, and she knew that she would never encounter anyone like Alessandro Zancani ever again.

The water taxi picked up a couple more passengers, then headed towards the Piazza San Marco landing stage.

It was where Francine had first set foot in Venice, yesterday evening. As she got off the boat, she tried to pretend that the hours in between had never happened, and she was arriving here for the very first time.

She really *had* to forget about last night, she told herself firmly. It was time to return to the real world, and pick up the threads of her life again.

But nothing seemed very real to her right now. She could still too clearly feel the echo of excitement, the ache of pleasure, the guilty thrill of the fantasy.

'Pretend that I'm your perfect lover, Francine,' Alessandro had murmured. And he had been—until she had suddenly panicked, and run. Every inch of his experienced body, every touch of his clever hands and sensual mouth, had been designed to give her pleasure. And he had succeeded!

Francine felt very shaky as she walked slowly across the Piazza San Marco. Despite her resolution to forget what had happened, every step reminded her of the similar journey she had made last night—and where it had led her. This time, though, she was determined not to make the same mistake. She stopped a couple of times to ask for directions to her hotel, and then followed them with almost obsessive care.

She eventually found the hotel without too much difficulty. Venice in bright sunlight was very different from the shadowed, mysterious, confusing place it had been last night. As soon as she walked into the lobby, she saw her boss's familiar face. Pete waved to her, and then came over.

'Good, you've arrived early,' he said briskly. 'Have you had a chance to grab some breakfast? Hurry and get something to eat, if you haven't. I want to make a really early start, before the tourists come out in force.'

'I don't want breakfast. And I'm sorry that I didn't arrive yesterday evening,' she apologised.

He waved his hand dismissively before she had time to launch into any explanations. 'I was out until late, but there was a garbled message from the receptionist when I got back. Some mix-up over your room, wasn't it? But you obviously found somewhere to stay for the night.'

'Er—yes,' Francine said cautiously.

To her relief, he didn't ask *where* she had stayed. Instead, he glanced at his watch. 'I've got the first location all lined up. It's a small canal quite near to the hotel, it'll only take us a few minutes to get there. I want the finished photographs to look like Renaissance paintings, richly coloured and textured. I've borrowed a whole set of medieval costumes for you to wear; they're hanging on a rack in my room, number twenty-three—here's the key. Will you go up to your room and get changed? Try the green or the gold dress, and leave your hair loose.'

Francine remembered the green silk dress she had worn last night. 'I'd rather not wear green,' she said, swallowing rather hard.

Pete didn't seem to notice her sudden discomfort. Once he started on a job, he concentrated totally on the work ahead.

'Because green's meant to be unlucky?' he said absently. 'I didn't know you were superstitious, Francine. But wear the gold dress, if that makes you feel happier.'

Francine wasn't at all sure that anything was going to make her feel happy today. If she was going to be of any use to Pete, though, she had to put on a bright smile and give him her full attention.

She signed in at Reception, collected her own key, and then ran quickly up to her room. She dumped her bag in the corner, and then stared at her reflection in the mirror.

She felt as if she ought to look different. Apart from a faint flush of colour on her cheeks, though, she looked just the same. Her wide green eyes were clear and alert, and her hair was its usual brilliant tangle of curls. Even her mouth showed no outward sign of bruising from those intense kisses.

Francine found herself licking her lips, as if searching for the faint, lingering taste of Alessandro. Just stop it! she ordered herself firmly. You've got work to do.

Professionally, she began to get herself ready for the photographs that Pete would soon be shooting. After a quick shower, she carefully applied much more make-up than she usually wore. She had watched the models that Pete used do it so often—and sometimes even helped them—that she knew exactly what was needed. A light foundation so that her skin glowed, but didn't shine, and then different colours, some subtle and some bright, to accentuate her eyes, lips, and fine cheekbones. Then she went along to Pete's room, to find the gold dress that he wanted her to wear.

She gave a faint groan when she discovered that it was made of a heavy, rich brocade with a deep, square neck, full sleeves extravagantly trimmed with lace, and a long, swirling skirt. Under the hot midsummer Venetian sun, she was going to melt!

After a few minutes of brushing and curling, her hair fell in a gold-red cascade around her shoulders. Francine studied the results critically, and then gave a small nod. Yes, she thought that was the look that Pete was aiming for.

She finally went back down to the lobby, feeling very self conscious in the elaborate gold dress. Pete was waiting for her, his photographic equipment stacked up around him. As she walked towards him, he glanced up and then did a double-take. Finally, a big grin spread over his face.

'That's really knock-'em-dead stuff! You're a great girl, Francine. You always give me what I want.'

'I'm going to feel a complete fool walking through the streets of Venice, dressed like this,' she said, wrinkling her nose.

'We haven't got far to go.' He began to pick up the bags that held his equipment, and slung them over his shoulder. Then he glanced over to her. 'That dress looks perfect, but I suppose you couldn't give me just a little more cleavage?' he said hopefully.

'No,' she said very firmly. The low-cut, square neck already showed quite enough of her!

'I thought not. But it was worth a try,' he said with a grin. 'Come on, let's get going.'

He headed out of the hotel, dived into the maze of back streets opposite, and began to thread his way through them with confidence. Francine trotted after him, grateful that there weren't too many people around yet to stare at her in this elaborate costume.

After several minutes, she saw the glimmer of water ahead, a small canal that shimmered gently in the sunshine.

'This is it,' Pete announced, and walked over to the narrow bridge that crossed the canal.

Francine stared at it, her pulses beginning to thump very hard. It looked disturbingly familiar. Perhaps a lot of the small bridges in Venice looked like this, she tried to comfort herself. But the steps leading up either side, the ornate lamp suspended from an elegant pole in the middle—she was almost certain this was where she had been last night. This was the very bridge where those two men had threatened her, and she had been rescued by Alessandro!

'Did you hear what I said, Francine?' Pete demanded with a touch of exasperation.

'What——?' she said edgily.

'I want you to stand in the very centre of the bridge, under the lamp. And try to look rather dreamy—as if you've just left your lover.'

Automatically, Francine obeyed, taking up her pose in the middle of the bridge. And the dreamy look wasn't too difficult—she was already beginning to feel as if she were sleepwalking!

'Very nice,' Pete said encouragingly. 'And the light is marvellous, clear and golden. Hold it while I take a few Polaroids.'

Like many photographers, Pete took Polaroid pictures first, so that he would have a rough idea what the finished photographs would look like. He shot a dozen, waited for them to develop, and then grunted in satisfaction.

'They look fine. OK, I'll set up the cameras and we'll go for the real thing.'

While he worked, Francine stood there like a statue, her red-gold hair dazzling in the sunshine and her skin already very hot. Her stomach gently churned as she found herself thinking about last night—about

Alessandro. And she had been so determined to put him right out of her mind! Here she was, though, back at the very spot where she had first met him. Pete couldn't possibly have known, of course, it was just a tremendous coincidence that he had picked this particular bridge for the first set of photographs. It was certainly making her feel very peculiar, though, to be standing here again.

Then Francine began to feel that she really *must* be dreaming—or even having a hallucination—because a tall, dark figure had suddenly appeared at the far end of the bridge. His face was half turned away from her, but everything about that powerful body looked heart-stoppingly familiar. She found that she was clutching the rail beside her very hard because her legs had suddenly gone dreadfully weak.

Pete walked over to the man and casually started talking to him. Francine couldn't hear what they were saying, only the indistinct murmur of their voices. Her heart was thudding so loudly that the heavy beat seemed to be echoing right through her head, and her hands were gently shaking.

She tried to convince herself that it wasn't Alessandro, it *couldn't* be him. Perhaps the whole scene really was just a figment of her imagination. She closed her eyes, squeezed them very hard, but when she found the courage to open them again, the tall dark figure was still there. And it definitely was Alessandro!

He had turned now, and was looking directly at her. Francine felt her legs turn completely to jelly. There were no dark shadows this morning, the sun was shining straight down on to his face and she could clearly see every small detail. The strong, dark features, the hard, sensual mouth, and skin that was deeply and evenly tanned. His eyes were grey this morning—then they suddenly glinted and turned green. And the scar that ran right across his cheekbone stood out starkly in the brilliant light, marring his arrogant features and giving them a devilish slant.

Francine swallowed convulsively. She had been so convinced that she would never see him again. And now that he was standing just a few yards away, she had no idea what to do or say.

At the same time, she could feel that small, hot ache in the pit of her stomach again. How could he do that to her, simply by standing there and looking at her? She had no idea, but she did know that it scared her half to death!

Pete turned to her and waved one hand. 'Francine, come over here for a couple of minutes.'

She didn't want to move. For a few seconds, she wasn't even sure that she *could* move. Then she managed to get her legs to work, and walked jerkily forward, her entire body feeling stiff and awkward.

Alessandro's grey-green eyes—such beautiful eyes, Francine realised with a deep shiver—never moved from her face. Pete didn't seem to notice how pale she had gone, and he smiled happily at her as she approached.

'Francine, this is Signor Alessandro Zancani,' he said. 'He's interested in my work. In fact, he thinks that I might be able to help him with a project he has in mind.'

Francine hardly heard what Pete was saying. Instead, she just kept looking at that dark, compelling face, as if hypnotised.

'Signor Zancani owns a company that sells high quality sportswear,' Pete went on enthusiastically. 'He's got a new range of designs on the drawing-board, and he's looking for a photographer to produce the pictures for a catalogue that will be distributed worldwide.'

'I would like to see examples of your work,' Alessandro said smoothly. 'Perhaps you could send me some prints of the photographs that you're taking today?'

'Certainly,' Pete agreed at once. 'These photos are for a calendar, they're quite different from the kind of work that you would be requiring, but I can also send you examples of other catalogue work that I've done.'

'This is the address of my company,' said Alessandro, handing him a crisp white card. 'If you send the photos directly there, they will reach me. Do you have a business manager with whom I could discuss financial details?'

'Oh, Francine handles the financial side of the business,' Pete said at once. 'This is Francine Allen,' he said, turning to her and introducing her formally.

Alessandro gave no indication that they had met before. And done a great deal more than simply meet! Francine realised that he hadn't spoken one word directly to her so far, he was treating her as if she were a complete stranger. What was going on here? And how was she supposed to respond?

'Francine can give you all the information you need, and even prepare a full quotation for you, if you decide that you like my work,' Pete was now saying.

'Really?' Alessandro murmured, his black brows gently lifting. 'I assumed that she was simply your model.'

And yet there was no real surprise in his voice. Francine was suddenly left with the odd impression that he knew exactly what part she played in Pete's small business. But that was impossible, she told herself. She hadn't told him anything about her job last night. In fact, she had hardly given him any personal information at all, except her name.

A moment later, she completely dismissed her suspicions. She wasn't important, she certainly wasn't famous, so how could he possibly know anything about her? What she really had to figure out was why he was behaving as if this were their very first meeting.

She didn't have any more time to think about it, though. Alessandro turned to her and finally spoke directly to her.

'Perhaps you and I could have a meeting, Francine, to discuss preliminary details.' His velvet voice seemed to gently mock her, and she was sure that she could see a challenge in his eyes, turning them as green as her own. 'You don't mind if I call you by your first name?' he added softly.

Francine longed to blurt out that he could call her absolutely anything he liked, as long as he said it in that low, dark voice that turned all of her limbs to jelly. Instead, she somehow managed to keep control of herself. For reasons of his own, he obviously didn't want Pete to know that they had met before. All right, she was willing to go along with that. In fact, she realised that she was willing to go along with just about anything if it meant that she could see him one more time.

'No, I don't mind, Signor Zancani,' she said, and it felt very odd to be addressing him so formally when all she could seem to think about right now was the way this man's mouth had explored the secrets of her body; the way his hands had——

She caught her breath and told herself to stop, *stop*, or she was going to go to pieces right here, in front of him!

Pete suddenly clicked his fingers. 'Alessandro Zancani,' he said. 'I knew that your name sounded familiar. You used to be a racing driver; you drove on the Formula One circuit.'

'That was several years ago,' Alessandro said indifferently.

'And what do you do now, Signor Zancani?' Francine asked.

His grey-green eyes fixed on her again, setting all of her nerves abruptly on edge. 'I make money,' he replied softly.

'That can't be as exciting as racing cars.'

'That depends on how you go about it. The business world can be just as dangerous and unpredictable as a race-track.'

'And you like danger?' she prompted him.

'I don't think that life should ever be boring.'

Francine was quite sure that boredom didn't figure in Alessandro Zancani's life at all! Then she realised that Pete was looking at the two of them rather curiously, as if trying to figure out what was going on. Alessandro's gaze moved smoothly over to him.

'I'm glad that we've had this chance meeting, and I'm sure that we can do business together. I look forward to discussing the details with Miss Allen.' His eyes swung back to fix on Francine. 'Perhaps we could meet at the Caffè Florian this evening? At seven o'clock?'

'Oh—er—yes,' she managed to get out, a little resentful of the way he was managing to keep so cool while she was a quivering mass of nerves.

'I look forward to it, Francine,' he murmured, and her heart performed what felt like a triple somersault as he said her name again. Then he nodded to Pete, and strode off.

Francine blinked dazedly, and even wondered for a few moments if she had dreamed the whole thing. Pete was looking extremely pleased with himself, though, grinning broadly as he set up his camera for the next shots.

'I think our luck's about to change,' he said enthusiastically. 'A commission from Alessandro Zancani could be just what we need to push us right to the top. I think that you're my good luck charm, Francine. Things always go well when you're around.'

'Alessandro Zancani,' she said slowly, secretly relishing the guilty pleasure of saying his name. 'What do you know about him?'

'Only what I've read,' Pete admitted. 'He used to race cars—and very successfully—but a major smash-up put a stop to that. He was out of racing for a long time, recovering from his injuries, and never went back to it.'

Francine bit her lip. 'What kind of injuries?'

'To his leg mainly, if I remember rightly. He obviously recovered completely, though; I didn't notice any trace of a limp.' Pete glanced up at her. 'Are you sure you haven't heard of him?'

She shook her head. 'The only sports I watch are tennis and athletics. I've never been interested in racing.'

'After he gave up Formula One, he went into business,' Pete went on. 'Sportswear and equipment, fitness studios, that kind of thing. And he promotes sporting events, brings together big names for huge fees. He's probably got a lot of other interests that no one even knows about, because he's obviously rolling in money. One of those men for whom everything turns into gold,' he finished a little enviously.

'You seem to know a lot about him,' Francine said curiously.

'I read an article about him just a short time ago,' Pete admitted. 'Pure coincidence, of course, I'd no idea that I'd actually be meeting him. If I remember rightly, the article was written without his co-operation, and it was mainly rumour and speculation. Even if only a quarter of the rumours were true, though, he's still clearly a guy who's tried everything once.'

'Then why is he thinking of giving that contract to *us*?' Francine wondered out loud. 'We're such a small outfit, and he must have contacts all over the world. He would only have to pick up the phone and he could have the very best.'

'We are one of the best,' Pete said firmly. 'It's just that we're the only ones who know that, so far!' Then, seeing she still looked doubtful, he went on, 'Look, perhaps he's just one of these guys who likes to give a chance to the underdog. A surprising number of top businessmen are prepared to do that. They've already made it, and they like to help someone else get their feet on that good old ladder of success. It makes them feel good. And it makes good business sense, as well, because they're obviously going to pay a lot less to an outfit like ours than someone already at the very top, yet they'll get a product that's just as good.'

'Are we really ready to compete with the top studios?' she said, her eyebrows shooting up.

'Of course we are,' Pete said without hesitation.

'And you really want to do business with Alessandro—er, Signor Zancani?' she hurriedly corrected herself. If she used Alessandro's Christian name too freely, Pete might begin to suspect something.

'Are you kidding?' Pete said in disbelief. 'I'd walk over fire to get a contract from someone like him! It could be the making of the business, Francine. He's got so many contacts, and all the power and influence that one man can handle. If we do a good job for him, it could bring us in so much work that we'd have to expand, take on more staff. As soon as we get back to England, I'm going to get together a portfolio of work that's so damned brilliant that he'll send us a contract by return of post! Just do a good job of sweet-talking him tonight, Francine, make sure that he stays interested in us until I can get those photos to him.'

'What do you mean?' she said suspiciously.

Pete gave her a quick grin. 'Come on, don't play the innocent. I saw the way he looked at you. I'd say it was love—or lust!—at first sight. We can use that, Francine. Just turn on the charm, bat those long eyelashes at him, make sure he doesn't forget us.'

'That's not the way we do business!' she said sharply.

'Just lately, we haven't been doing much business at all,' he reminded her. 'We need to take advantage of every break that comes our way.' Then, seeing the rather fierce look on her face, he went on more placatingly, 'I'm not telling you to jump straight into bed with him. All it needs is a few seductive smiles while you're telling him that I'm an absolutely brilliant photographer, and the one man who can give him the catalogue of his dreams.'

'You're impossible,' she said in exasperation.

'I know,' he said, grinning again. 'But face it, Francine, you *are* sexy.' He hesitated for a moment, then went on, 'Shall I tell you a secret? There have been times when you've certainly turned *me* on. I've always stopped myself from doing anything about it, though, because I knew that we wouldn't be able to work together afterwards.'

Francine stared at him in amazement. 'I didn't know——'

'Don't worry about it,' Pete said wryly. 'I can live with a little frustration. I'm only telling you so that you know why I sometimes go rather red and hurry out of the room when you get too close to me!' Then his face became unexpectedly sober. 'To be more serious, Francine, it really is time that you took more notice of the effect you have on men. It could be dangerous to go on waltzing through life as if you were a Plain Jane whom no one noticed. It could lead to some very unpleasant surprises.'

Francine found herself suddenly swallowing hard, because she had already discovered some of the surprises that men were capable of. Last night had certainly been the biggest surprise of her life! And in just a few hours, she would meet Alessandro Zancani again.

She was already wondering if she had the nerve to go through with the meeting. And, if she did, what would it lead to?

CHAPTER FOUR

FOR Francine, the rest of the day passed incredibly slowly. She glanced at her watch dozens of times, convinced that it must actually have stopped. She took no notice of the small crowds of tourists who gathered to watch Pete taking his photographs, and she didn't even feel the sun beating down on her uncovered head, turning her hair into a blaze of colour.

She certainly *did* feel her pulses thumping with excitement as the time for her next meeting with Alessandro finally drew nearer.

When Pete had finally taken his last shot, she dashed back to the hotel, yanked off the gold dress and dived under the shower. She left her hair to dry in tousled curls around her shoulders as she frantically sorted through the small amount of luggage she had brought with her. Why, oh, why hadn't she packed at least one outfit that was glitzy and glamorous? she asked herself almost in despair, as she hunted through the bright, casual clothes that filled her bag.

Then a dark shadow in the corner caught her eye, and with a small sigh of relief she pulled out the absolutely plain black dress that she must have chucked in at the very last moment. She didn't even remember packing it, although she usually took it everywhere because it was such a useful item. It was a go-anywhere kind of dress, stretchy so that it clung to the generous curves of her body, and her hair always looked dazzling against its darkness.

Francine glanced at her watch for the umpteenth time, and then hurriedly wriggled into the dress. Her face needed only the very minimum of make-up; her skin already glowed from her day spent standing in the sun—and from nervous excitement!

A touch of shadow on her eyelids made her green eyes look more mysterious—she hoped!—a light brushing of mascara darkened her long, thick lashes and a hint of colour outlined the soft, perfect shape of her mouth.

Then she sorted through the small box of jewellery she had brought with her, thinking that some of it might be needed for the photographs. She found a chunky necklace which jazzed up the plain black dress, and finally she twisted her unruly hair into a gleaming knot on top of her head, leaving just a few bright tendrils to drift around her long, slim neck.

Finally, she was ready to go. She was so very nervous that her throat was completely dry. Was she absolutely mad, she wondered, to see this man again? But she suddenly knew that she couldn't bear *not* to see him, at least one more time.

It wasn't far from the hotel to the Piazza San Marco. She pushed her way through the crowds of people wandering around the huge square, to the Caffè Florian. Tables were set outside, and a small orchestra played, competing with the noise of the crowds in the Piazza and the orchestra of the Caffè Quadri on the other side of the square.

Francine's eyes were already fixed on Alessandro, though. He was sitting at one of the tables outside, and he was dressed far more formally than most of the people around him, in a dark suit and gleaming white shirt. His black hair and the scar across his face gave him a rakish air, and as Francine walked towards him on legs that had suddenly become precariously unsteady, she became aware that other women were interested in him. *Very* interested; some of them were quite blatantly trying to attract his attention.

Alessandro was looking only at her, though. Francine very nearly stopped breathing as his intense gaze swept over her. He swiftly got to his feet as she approached, but when she went to sit opposite him, he moved forward and took hold of her arm.

'I've booked a table inside,' he told her. 'It'll be quieter, more private. We'll be able to talk.'

The touch of his fingers against her bare arm set off a dozen different sensations inside her, all of them deliciously pleasant. Francine let him lead her inside, into one of the Florian's small inner rooms with dark red banquettes, gold cornices, and the famous paintings under glass.

A waiter appeared as soon as they had sat down, and Alessandro ordered for both of them. Afterwards, though, Francine couldn't remember what she had eaten or drunk. What she could very clearly remember was the sound of Alessandro's voice, seductively dark and soft. He spoke about the history of Venice, the great days of trade when ships filled with spices and perfumes and silks sailed into the lagoon, and the city ruled over vast territories. And he talked of the modern-day problems, the rising water-levels which were causing such concern—and structural damage—and the everyday problems of a city which, in summer, was filled to absolute capacity with tourists.

When they finally left Florian's, darkness had fallen. Alessandro walked with her back to her hotel, and, as they stood outside, Francine found herself biting her lip.

'We—we didn't talk about business at all this evening,' she said rather jerkily. 'And that was why we had dinner—wasn't it?'

Alessandro smiled. 'Of course it was. I'm afraid that means we shall just have to meet again. Tomorrow at one, for lunch?' he suggested softly. 'At Harry's Bar?'

She was dying to say yes, *yes*. She forced herself to keep her voice casual, though. 'I'm not sure—I'll have to check with Pete, my boss——'

'Oh, I think that Pete will agree,' he said, his eyes briefly glittering. 'Especially since he's obviously hoping for a contract with my company.'

'Are you going to let him take the photographs for your catalogue?' she asked directly.

He looked at her consideringly. 'Do you think that I should?'

'Yes, definitely yes. He's very good, he really is,' she said earnestly.

'I think that this is something that needs to be discussed at length,' Alessandro said, his gaze now resting on her in a way that made her skin prickle quite deliciously. 'In fact, it may take several meetings. I hope that you don't have any other plans for your spare time this week?'

'No, I don't,' she said at once, and then immediately wanted to kick herself for sounding so eager. Play it cool, she reminded herself. This man must be used to women falling over themselves to do whatever he suggests. You don't want to be just one more of a large crowd. You want——

Francine caught her breath as she realised just what she wanted. To be special. *Very* special. Just twenty-four hours after meeting this man, she already wanted the impossible.

Alessandro lightly took hold of her hand, and his lips softly brushed against the back of her fingers. The old-fashioned gesture seemed entirely right in this unique city that still seemed to be rooted in the past. There was nothing in the least old-fashioned about the way he made her feel, though. Sheer desire trembled inside her, and from the sudden brilliance of his eyes she knew that it was reciprocated.

She was aware of a sudden surge of triumph. It made her feel completely female, to be so easily able to arouse such an experienced man.

'Tomorrow at one,' Alessandro reminded her, his gaze now fixed on her face.

Francine knew that there was no chance she would forget. She felt as if she were going to remember every single minute she spent with Alessandro for the rest of her life.

She waited tensely for him to kiss her, she was so sure that he wouldn't be able to leave without touching her again. He simply stood there, though, his entire body tense, as if he gained a strange pleasure from looking but not touching. Then, with a small nod, he swung round and strode off.

Francine went slowly into the hotel, feeling peculiarly empty inside. Had she been completely wrong about everything? Was she only imagining the spark that seemed to leap into life whenever she was near him? Why hadn't he kissed her properly again?

She tossed and turned restlessly for most of the night, impatiently posed for Pete most of the morning, wearing another heavy medieval costume which made her very hot and uncomfortable in the blazing heat of the Venetian sun. Then it was finally lunchtime, and there was just time to whizz into the hotel and change before dashing off to Harry's Bar, to meet Alessandro.

Her first glimpse of his face convinced her that she *hadn't* been wrong last night. His grey-green eyes flared brightly as she walked towards him, and the hard line of his mouth relaxed, became fuller and more sensual.

Francine was so relieved that she chattered nervously all through lunch, and time fled by. Pete had only given her an hour's break, and she was terrified that she had wasted it. What if Alessandro had simply been bored by all that gabbled conversation?

Her knees actually sagged with relief when he made another date for dinner the next day. And the day after that. In fact, it seemed that he wanted to see her every day that she remained in Venice.

They always met in public, though, he never took her back to the palazzo again. Because he didn't quite trust himself? Francine wondered with a small flare of excitement.

Slowly, she learnt more about him. She discovered that his father had been Italian and his mother English, although both of his parents had been dead for several years. He had always lived in Italy, but had been educated in England and visited it frequently, and he felt equally at home in both countries.

He didn't seem to want to talk about his days as a racing driver. Francine guessed that that part of his life had already been fully documented in newspapers, magazines and books. If she wanted to know about it, she only had to read about it, and she planned to do just that, as soon as she had the chance.

Towards the end of the week, she finally found the courage to ask him about the scar on his face.

'Did it happen in the smash-up on the race-track?' she asked a little tentatively. At the same time, she gave a small shiver at the thought of the crash that had put an end to his career in racing.

Alessandro lightly ran one finger down the scar. 'No,' he said, after a long silence. 'It happened years before that. I was wild when I was young,' he went on, with a sudden, dark frown. 'There was a fight; it turned into a matter of honour over something that was said about my family. It became rather savage, and we both had knives——'

Francine couldn't quite suppress a shudder, but Alessandro kept his own voice very controlled as he went on, 'My mother cried when she saw my face, but my father simply told me that I had learned a valuable lesson. That only stupid men fight with weapons when there are so many other, more suitable ways of inflicting damage. He said that the most effective way of hurting people was to damage them financially or emotionally, and that he would teach me how to do both. He then beat me for getting involved in a knife fight, and refused to let the doctors use plastic surgery to disguise the scar. He wanted me to remember, every time I looked at myself, that physical violence was not the way to exact revenge.'

Her green eyes had grown wide with sheer disbelief. 'How could someone do that to their own son? It's barbaric. So cruel!'

Alessandro merely shrugged. 'It's often a cruel world that we live in, and it's best to learn at an early age how to survive in it.'

Despite his cool voice, though, Francine suspected that the memory of that time still haunted him. There had been something in his tone, almost too controlled, and his face, carefully expressionless, that betrayed the truth. She also realised that she was glad Alessandro's father was now dead and she wouldn't have to meet him.

She found herself telling him about her own family. 'My mother and father were divorced when I was quite young. I don't know why they ever married in the first place,' she went on frankly. 'They live in two such completely different worlds that they must have known from the very beginning that it would be quite impossible for them to live together for very long. And I'm quite sure that *I* was a mistake. They were probably horrified when I turned up to complicate things even further. My mother was given custody of me after the divorce, although to be honest I didn't see very much of her. I was brought up by grandparents, aunts, uncles, anyone who was willing to have me for a few months.'

'And your father?' Alessandro said, his eyes unexpectedly dark and intense.

'He went back to America after the divorce. He's English, but he's lived over there for most of his life. He's a marvellous man,' she said affectionately, 'but just no good at family life. That was about the only thing he and my mother had in common,' she added very wryly. 'My mother's an artist—she paints and sculpts, and she travels all round the world in search of inspiration. She's in India at the moment. At least, I think she is. I haven't heard from her for a couple of months, she isn't very good at keeping in touch, so she might have moved on by now. And my father——'

Here, Francine hesitated, because the subject of her father was a little delicate. Only her closest friends, and Pete, her boss, knew who her father actually was. It was the way that she and her father preferred it; she, because she was very independent and didn't ever want to be accused of trading on her father's name, and her father because he didn't want it to become public knowledge that he had a daughter who was twenty-one years old. His Press handouts gave his age as 'mid-thirties', but if everyone knew that he had a grown-up daughter, they would certainly begin to suspect that 'late forties' was a far more accurate guess. And for a film actor who had made a career out of playing romantic leads, that would have been rather a handicap. An enterprising journalist might even have dug further and found out about the discreet surgery that had kept the lines on his face at bay, the highlighted hair, and the long, arduous hours in the gym that were now necessary to keep his body hard muscled and slim.

Alessandro leant forward, his grey-green eyes still rivetted on her face. 'Tell me about your father,' he invited softly.

Francine realised that she didn't want to keep anything back. She wanted him to know everything about her.

'My father is Paul James,' she admitted. 'You must have heard of him. He's never made it into the really big time, but he's been in dozens of TV films and mini-series which sell all round the world, and he's very well known.' She gave a wry smile. 'And his lifestyle hits the headlines fairly regularly, as well. He's always been a great believer in the old saying about any publicity being better than none. Not much of it is faked, either; he really is a larger-than-life kind of person, always ready for new experiences and wanting to try absolutely everything at least once.'

For just an instant, Alessandro's eyes flickered very brightly, as if something had just touched a raw nerve. Then they grew cool again, and rather remote.

'I rarely watch television,' he said. 'And I'm certainly not interested in the gossip columns. Your father's name means nothing to me. Do you see him very often?'

She gave a small sigh. 'Not as often as I'd like. If he's filming in England or Europe, I try and meet up with him, and I've been to America a few times. I haven't seen him for several months, though, or even spoken to him on the phone for the last few weeks. He's filming in some inaccessible spot in South America at the moment, he won't be back in the States until some time next month.'

Alessandro nodded slowly, and she had the feeling that her answer pleased him. Why would her father's absence give him satisfaction, though?

Because then you can give *him* your undivided attention? said a small, hopeful voice inside her head.

Francine quickly told herself not to be fanciful. She couldn't stop the sudden accelerated beat of her pulses, though.

Her last couple of days in Venice slid past, taking on an almost dreamlike quality. The heat, the time she spent with Alessandro, the small, constant ache of desire inside her body, the faded splendour of Venice itself, all combined to make her feel constantly off balance, hot, languid, a stranger to herself. And yet, she liked feeling this way. She didn't want this strange experience ever to end.

It was with an acute sense of shock that she woke up one morning and realised that Pete had almost finished shooting his photographs. They would be flying home tomorrow.

That evening, she met with Alessandro for the last time at the Caffè Florian, in the same small, exquisitely decorated room as on that first evening. It was an oasis of quiet in the swirl of noise and movement that filled the Piazza San Marco, and they ate in silence, although Francine could only pick at her meal.

'You're not hungry?' Alessandro said, at last.

'Not really,' she admitted, pushing her plate away.

'You don't want to leave Venice tomorrow.' It was a statement, not a question.

'No, I don't want to go,' she admitted softly.

'I'm also leaving Venice in the morning.'

Surprise—and a small wave of shock—rolled through her. She fought hard to prevent it appearing on her face, afraid of revealing far too much.

'You're going away?' she asked, trying to sound casual, but failing miserably.

'On a business trip, to Hong Kong and the Far East.'

'Will you——?' She swallowed hard, and tried again to keep her voice cool and steady. 'Will you be gone for long?'

'Just a few days. I'll be back in Venice next week. You could meet me here,' he suggested quietly.

Her head jerked up, sending her bright hair flying out in all directions. 'Meet you?' she echoed, suddenly full of new hope.

His mouth relaxed into a wickedly seductive smile. 'If you want to.'

'Oh, yes,' she breathed. 'Yes, I do!'

Satisfaction gleamed momentarily in Alessandro's eyes, turning them pure green.

'Will you keep in touch while you're away?' Francine asked with sudden shyness.

'No.' His blunt reply made her own eyes fly wide open, and his hand slid over to cover hers, his fingers playing briefly against her own, sending delicious sensations rocketing across her palms. 'I want you to have some time on your own,' he went. 'You need to think things over. To be very sure.'

'Sure of what?' she asked, her heart thumping very hard, now.

'What you want.'

'I already know——' she began at once, but he held up his hand to silence her.

'Things might seem very different when you're back home, in familiar surroundings. But I want you to make me a very firm promise. I don't want you to discuss our relationship with anyone, not even your family or closest friends. Whatever decision you finally make, I want it to be *yours*. Promise me that,' he ordered, his eyes suddenly fierce.

'I promise,' she said obediently. At the same time, excitement rushed through her. He had talked about their relationship as if it were to be a long-term thing.

Alessandro's gaze remained locked on to hers, not allowing her to look away from him for a single second. 'Then a week today you'll either come back to Venice—and me—or you'll stay away forever.'

She suddenly bit her lip. 'What if I come and—and *you've* changed your mind,' she said with a quick rush of apprehension. It was so hard to believe that he was actually saying these things to her; that he could mean them.

A strange expression crossed Alessandro's face. 'I made my mind up a long time ago. I won't change it.'

What on earth did he mean by that? Francine wondered dizzily, her head still spinning from all the implications of everything he had said. Had he known what he wanted since that very first night at the palazzo? But that was hardly a long time ago. Unless it seemed to him—as it did to her—that they had already known each other half a lifetime.

He didn't allow her to ask any more questions. Instead, he led her out of the café, his fingers lightly but firmly locked around her arm. They walked back to her hotel without saying another word, and when they reached it, Francine waited in hungry anticipation for the light, seductive brush of his lips against her fingers.

Instead, though, Alessandro pulled her almost roughly towards him, bent his head and kissed her full on the mouth. It wasn't a soft or gentle kiss. It was as fierce as the kisses he had given her on that first night at the palazzo, and Francine felt her body first sag with relief at the longed for intimate contact, and then strain a little frantically towards him, already wanting more.

He was more than willing to give it. He locked her tight against him so that his heart hammered against her crushed breasts, his body clearly told her that he already wanted her. His tongue explored the softness of her mouth quite ruthlessly, and his hands began to slide over the thin material of her dress, searching out the small, hidden pleasure spots.

Francine became lost in just seconds, she couldn't even remember where she was. Her fingers ached to touch him, she was amazed at her own boldness, and he groaned with pleasure for a few moments, then reluctantly held her hand away.

'This is a public street,' he reminded her, his mouth twisting into a wry line. His voice was breathless, though, and an instant later he pulled her further back into the shadows and began a new assault on her mouth.

Francine wasn't completely naïve, and she had thought that she knew all there was to know about kissing. Alessandro swiftly made her realise that she knew nothing at all!

One moment, his mouth was soft and seductive, the next he demanded total surrender, his lips so hard and fierce that they bruised her. It was a delicious bruising, though, and she didn't want it ever to end.

Then the street, which had been deserted, began to come noisily to life again as a small crowd of people poured into it from the far end. Alessandro took a couple of deep breaths and eased her away from him.

'You've just a few days to make your decision, Francine,' he said roughly. 'I won't wait any longer.'

He gave her one last, swift kiss; then he turned and strode off, leaving her hot and shaking, her mind and body whirling turbulently with a whole flood of emotions and desires.

She wanted to run after him immediately, tell him that she didn't need even one day, she could give him her answer right now. But something held her back, the small voice of common sense somehow breaking through the storm of emotion Alessandro had whipped up. This was a decision that she needed to make on her home ground, when she was calmer, more in control; when she could think straight. If she was ever going to be able to think straight again!

In the morning, she and Pete left for the airport, leaving behind a Venice that was hot, golden, crowded, noisy and, for Francine, full of sensual memories. She supposed that she was behaving fairly normally. When Pete spoke to her, she managed to answer without subsiding into total gibberish. He did give her an odd, enquiring look now and again, but to her relief he didn't ask any awkward questions.

She had thought that, once she was back home, everything that had happened to her in Venice would begin to take on a dreamlike quality, but it didn't. Every memory stayed crystal-clear and vivid in her mind; when she closed her eyes she could still feel the touch of Alessandro's lips, the heat of his skin, the touch of his fingers against her body. She could hear his voice, see those intense grey-green eyes, picture the scar that marred his otherwise perfect features.

Then Francine would begin to tremble gently inside, because it was frightening to feel so close, so intimately connected, to someone she had only known for a few days. It was a holiday romance, she tried to convince herself. Just a holiday romance. The only trouble was, it felt terrifyingly like love.

When Pete developed the photographs he had shot of her in Venice for the calendar, he was delighted with them. When Francine saw them, she understood why. The faded splendour of the sunlit backdrops, the rich tones of the costumes she had worn, the bright halo of her hair, all combined to produce photos that were deeply romantic and glowing with sensual colours. And something in the expression on her face, the slightly feverish light in her eyes, gave them an added evocative quality.

Pete put the prints down on the table, then turned and looked at her.

'You're going back there, aren't you?' he said bluntly. 'To Venice, to Alessandro Zancani.'

She knew that the shock showed clearly on her face. 'How—how did you know?' she got out.

'Francine, I'm not stupid and I'm not blind,' he said drily, and she felt herself blushing.

'Is it that obvious?' she said with some embarrassment.

'Only to someone who knows you well,' Pete said more kindly. 'Am I going to lose you permanently?'

'I don't know. I don't even understand what's going on; it's like being hit with a sledgehammer,' she admitted. 'I never expected anything like this to happen to me, and now that it has I don't even know how to handle it.'

'But you are going to see Alessandro Zancani again?'

'I can't imagine *not* seeing him. I don't know if I'm doing the right thing—probably not; it's really crazy when you stop and think about it. But I've got to go.'

'When?' he asked.

'Next week. I was going to ask you if I could have a few days off,' she said in a small voice.

'If I say no, you'll still go, won't you?' he said with some resignation.

'Yes,' she said, without even stopping to think about it.

His face grew more serious. 'Just be careful, Francine,' he said in a sombre tone. 'This man is quite unlike anyone you've ever known before. Even your father doesn't measure up to him in any way.'

Her brows drew together in a brief frown. 'Are you warning me about him?'

'No, I don't think so,' Pete said slowly. 'I'm only saying that perhaps you shouldn't rush into anything too fast.'

'I think it might be too late for that,' she said wryly. 'But thanks for being concerned about me. And because you've been such a great boss, I'm going to take you out for an expensive lunch—my treat,' she added, smiling at him with a great rush of affection.

'Why do I get the feeling that this is a goodbye meal?' Pete said, with a deep sigh. 'And where am I ever going to find another assistant as brilliant as you've been?'

'Don't write me off yet,' Francine said more soberly. 'I might be making the biggest mistake of my life. I might even be on the first plane back from Venice.'

Inside, though, she was already quite sure that she wouldn't be coming back. And her heart was thumping away at breakneck speed, at the thought of seeing Alessandro again.

But if he wants you to stay, what will you be? asked a small voice inside her head. His girlfriend? His mistress?

Francine didn't know. She told herself that she didn't even care, and ordered the voice to shut up.

The next couple of days absolutely crawled by, and she became increasingly feverish with excitement and anticipation. Her ticket was booked, her bags were packed, and all she wanted to do was to get on the plane.

Pete drove her to the airport. As Francine hopped impatiently up and down, waiting for her flight to be called, he looked at her quizzically.

'No last-minute doubts?' he said.

'None,' she said firmly, ignoring the dozens of doubts that were gnawing away inside of her. 'As long as the flight isn't delayed, I'll be in Venice by lunchtime.'

'I hope everything works out the way you want it to,' he said sincerely. 'You know that I've got a temporary assistant to stand in for you, while you're away. Ring me and let me know if I'm going to need her permanently.'

'I will,' she promised. 'And thanks for everything, Pete. You've been a great friend, as well as a great boss.'

He actually blushed, which made both of them laugh. Then they suddenly hugged each other. Francine found herself almost wishing that she could have fallen for Pete. They had made such a great team and got on so well together, she always felt relaxed and comfortable with him. She had certainly never felt relaxed when she was with Alessandro! But he could make her feel a hundred other things that were so much more exciting.

Her flight was finally called and she hurried on board. She had kept her promise to Alessandro and told no one, except Pete, that she was returning to Venice. If any of her friends rang, they would simply find a message on her answerphone saying she had gone away for a few days. She might not have been able to stop herself confiding in one of her parents, if they had been around, but her father was still filming in a remote part of South America, and her mother was somewhere in Nepal. Francine had had a postcard a couple of days ago, with just a few scribbled lines on it enthusing about the ideas her mother was getting for a new series of paintings based on local traditional designs. Francine had given a small sigh, and briefly wondered what it would be like to have two ordinary parents!

She fidgeted restlessly all through the flight, and her stomach cramped with nervousness when the plane at last touched down at Marco Polo airport. Would Alessandro be at the palazzo? Would he still want her back again? Or had some other woman—perhaps the beautiful Gisella?—distracted his attention in the meantime, and made him forget how much he had wanted the girl with the red-gold hair he had found in his bed on that first sultry Venetian night?

She took a water taxi from the airport to Venice, which was ruinously expensive, but she didn't care. As it crossed the lagoon, she could see the outline of the city etched against the skyline, and her nervousness and excitement grew until she could scarcely breathe.

Then the taxi entered the Grand Canal, with the familiar sights sliding by in the brilliant sunshine that still washed over the city. Francine's eyes locked on to the palazzos that lined the canal until the one that she was searching for finally came into sight. The small jetty outside was deserted, though, and her heart felt as if it had just plummeted several feet. Alessandro wasn't looking out for her; wasn't waiting for her.

A couple of minutes later, she was standing on the jetty with her luggage piled up beside her. She stared at the closed door that led into the palazzo. Should she open it? Oh, God, what if it was *locked*?

But then the door opened silently of its own accord, and suddenly Alessandro was standing there. His grey-green eyes locked on to her face, and they suddenly glittered with a fleeting but vivid wave of emotion that she couldn't quite interpret. Triumph? Satisfaction? Swiftly suppressed anticipation?

'You came, *cara*,' he said softly.

Then he smiled at her, and suddenly everything seemed all right. He picked up her luggage and took it into the palazzo, and Francine stumbled after him. She had forgotten how just the sight of him could make her legs weaken quite disastrously!

Neither of them said a word as they climbed the stairs that took them up to the magnificently decorated first floor. Alessandro led her into a drawing-room that she hadn't seen before, its wide windows opening on to a breathtaking view of the Grand Canal. It was a comfortable room, though, despite the silk-covered walls, the great, engraved mirrors, the elegantly painted ceilings, the tables covered with chinoiserie, and the dazzling chandeliers. There were wide, plump sofas, arching palms with elegant leaves in soft green, and subtly coloured carpets. A room to relax in—except that Francine had never felt less relaxed in her entire life.

Alessandro turned to face her. 'You've brought plenty of luggage,' he said, his grey-green gaze raking over her, as if reminding himself of every small detail of how she looked. 'Have you come to stay?'

'Yes,' she said in a shaky voice. 'If that's what you want.'

'That's exactly what I want.' Again, there was that strange gleam of hidden triumph in his eyes. For just a moment, Francine felt a sudden wave of deep uncertainty sweep over her. Why was he looking at her like that? Was this some kind of game he was playing? Or a horrible joke?

His next words blasted away those thoughts, though. And they also left her in a state of total shock!

'There's just time for you to shower and find something suitable to wear,' Alessandro told her. 'I've arranged for us to be married at two o'clock.'

Francine knew that she was staring at him like a total idiot, but she couldn't help it. She couldn't believe he had just said that! She must have misheard him, or perhaps she was dreaming. Or even hallucinating!

'*Married?*' she managed to croak at last.

Alessandro moved a little closer, and his fingers lightly stroked the back of her hand. 'It's what we both want, isn't it?' he murmured.

'But I didn't think—I had no idea—we can't, things have to be arranged,' she gabbled almost incoherently. 'Oh, it's just not possible,' she finally finished, in breathless confusion.

'It's completely possible. The banns have been called; everything is ready.'

'But guests—dresses and flowers—witnesses——' she said helplessly. 'And I'd have to tell my family. My friends, Pete, would all want to be there. It would all take so much time——'

'No family, no friends,' Alessandro cut in. His gaze caught hers and relentlessly held it. 'Just you and I, Francine. You can wear one of my sister's dresses. Isn't it an English tradition to wear something borrowed at your wedding?' he reminded her softly.

'Yes, but—*how* can it all be arranged?' she said, still not quite believing any of this was really happening. 'You must need papers——'

'Only your passport. When you were first in Venice, I went to your hotel one day while you were out, and borrowed it.'

'That must be illegal.'

'Quite illegal,' he agreed. 'And so were a few of the other things I did. But I have some influence here, and it's surprising how helpful people are willing to be in the cause of true love.'

Was that a faint note of mockery in his voice? No, it couldn't be, Francine decided dazedly. No one would go to so much trouble unless they were very serious.

'When did you do all this?' she asked in a completely bemused voice.

'A couple of days after I first met you.'

'You knew so soon?'

'I knew that first night,' Alessandro replied, his answer taking her breath away. Then he glanced at his watch. 'Time's passing, Francine. In just an hour and a half, it will be two o'clock.' His gaze was still locked on to hers, brilliant and intense. 'You have to decide right now. Do you want to marry me?'

CHAPTER FIVE

FRANCINE wanted to shout out yes, *yes*! It took an enormous effort to make herself listen to the small, cautious voice inside her head warning her that it couldn't possibly be that simple, there had to be a dozen—a hundred—reasons why she couldn't do this crazy, marvellous, head-spinning thing.

'We really don't know each other very well,' she got out at last, looking at him anxiously because she certainly didn't want him to think that she was rejecting him outright.

'We'll discover everything that we need to know afterwards,' Alessandro told her huskily. His eyes glittered briefly. 'I'm very much looking forward to that.'

Francine gulped. So was she! 'Do you——?' Her throat seized up with sheer nerves and it was several seconds before she could finally finish the sentence. 'Do you love me?' she managed to say with almost crippling shyness.

'Love?' There was an odd, mocking note in his voice as he said the word, and she had the awful feeling that he was going to laugh at her naïve question. Then he seemed to realise that his reaction was not what she had been hoping for—longing for—and his hard mouth relaxed into a sensual smile. At the same time, his fingers drifted slowly up her bare arm, sending a whole army of goosebumps marching ahead of them.

'I love your skin,' he told her, his voice becoming a velvet smooth caress. 'It's warm and soft, and smells sweet. I love your breasts, the way that they swell under my fingers. I love the flatness of your stomach and the long, beautiful line of your legs. And the way your bright curls wind themselves around my fingers——'

Francine was finding it very hard to breathe by now, and she almost forgot that he hadn't answered her question. Almost, but not quite.

'I really need to know how you feel about *me*,' she managed to whisper, 'not just—just——'

'Not just your body?' Alessandro finished for her softly. His hand became still. 'I'll tell you exactly how I feel about you,' he promised. 'But only after the wedding.' His gaze locked on to hers. 'If you really want to know the truth, you'll have to marry me.' A hot light showed in his eyes, and he seemed to be very tense, as if filled with fierce emotions that he was barely keeping under control.

That voice inside Francine's head was still trying to warn her that this was too fast; not quite right. If she had any sense, she would tell him that she needed more time.

But she was terrified that he wouldn't be prepared to wait. If she said no, he might simply walk away. He had a lot of pride; he wouldn't take any kind of rejection easily.

Francine knew that she couldn't bear that to happen. She wanted this man in every kind of way she could think of. She wanted the pleasure of slowly getting to know everything about him, and sharing all the delicious kinds of intimacy with him. On that very first night at the palazzo she had fallen completely under his spell, and she had been bewitched and bedazzled—and in love—ever since.

She took a very deep breath. 'Yes, I'll marry you,' she said in a voice that was amazingly clear and firm.

Afterwards, she could never clearly remember the next couple of hours. She knew that she must have chosen an outfit from the wardrobe of Alessandro's sister, because she went to her wedding wearing a wickedly expensive dress in the very palest of cream. The skirt of the dress was plain silk, and the bodice covered with the most delicate, hand-made lace. Francine found shoes to match in a size so near to her own that they were only slightly tight, and tiny emerald studs to wear in her ears, the green as deep and sparkling as her eyes.

It felt strange to be getting married in another woman's clothes. Even stranger to think of it happening without any of her family or friends to witness the most important day of her life. And the strangest thing of all was that, in just a very short time, Alessandro Zancani would be her husband!

Francine felt hollow inside with nerves and excitement. Quite suddenly, she felt a desperate need to see at least one familiar face.

'Where's Angelina?' she asked Alessandro. His warm, friendly housekeeper was just the kind of person who could give her the support and encouragement that she needed right now.

'She's gone away for a few days,' Alessandro told her. 'I gave her some time off. I wanted us to be quite alone,' he finished, his eyes gleaming pure green.

Francine tried to convince herself it was all right, Alessandro was the most important person in her life right now; it didn't matter that Angelina wasn't here. That no one else at all was here.

Alessandro led her down to the jetty at the back of the palazzo, where a gondola was waiting them. Romance with a capital 'R', Francine told herself shakily, as she stepped into it. She rememberd how she had wished, on her very first day in Venice, that she could afford a ride in a gondola. Here she was, just a couple of weeks later, going to her *wedding* in one!

She settled back into the soft, velvet cushions, and felt her pulses thunder away even faster as Alessandro's fingers locked lightly around her own. Was he holding on to her to stop her running away, if she suffered a last-minute attack of nerves? she wondered, suppressing a nervous giggle.

Francine had to admit that part of her *did* want to run. This was an absolutely enormous step she was taking, and she was half excited, half terrified.

She glanced shyly at Alessandro, who looked magnificently impressive in an immaculately cut dark suit and crisp white shirt, with gold cuff links glittering at his wrists in the sunlight. His face, as always, had that arrogant expression that comes from supreme self confidence, and was stunningly distinctive with that deep scar ripping across his golden skin. His grey-green eyes looked fierce and intense, and glowed very brightly, as if lit by emotions barely kept in check.

Emotions caused by *her*? Francine thought wonderingly. She didn't dare ask, and realised how little she knew of what really went on inside that handsome head. Yet he certainly wanted to marry her. In fact, it seemed that he had wanted it from the moment he had first seen her. Which meant that he *must* love her, even though he hadn't yet said the actual words.

She remembered that he had promised to tell her exactly how he felt about her after the wedding. She felt a hot glow of anticipation, and knew that it would be hard to wait. Perhaps when she heard him say those magic words she would finally believe that this wasn't all some wonderful, fantastic dream.

Everything became even more blurred in her memory after that. She recalled standing in front of the mayor in his green, white and red sash, but understood very little of what he was saying. Two witnesses appeared, people she didn't recognise but who nodded deferentially to Alessandro, and Alessandro murmured a translation of the important parts of the ceremony. Francine almost stopped breathing as they exchanged rings. A gold band was placed on her finger, and a matching ring glinted on Alessandro's hand. Then there was another short speech from the mayor, and she finally heard him say, '*Siete marito e moglie.*'

'You are husband and wife.'

Wide-eyed with pure happiness, she turned to Alessandro. He looked back at her, but instead of the tenderness she had hoped to see, there was an expression of undisguised triumph on his face. He's just pleased that everything went so smoothly, she told herself. She waited in anticipation for the kiss that traditionally followed a wedding ceremony, but it didn't happen. Instead, Alessandro turned away from her to thank the two witnesses.

Perhaps it isn't the custom in Italy, Francine told herself in deep disappointment. With all the formalities over, she followed Alessandro out into the bright sunshine, expecting to see the gondola ready to take them back to the palazzo.

Instead, a water taxi was waiting for them. As she stepped into it, Francine saw her luggage was loaded on board.

She looked up at Alessandro in surprise. 'Where are we going?'

'To my villa, near Asolo,' he replied. 'Once we reach the mainland, it's only an hour's drive. It's very beautiful there, and very secluded—the perfect place for the kind of honeymoon I have in mind,' he finished, his eyes darkening.

Something in his tone of voice disturbed her, although she couldn't explain why. Then she shook off the feeling. The emotional tension of the day had probably affected him, as much as it had done her. Although, being a man, he would never admit it!

The water taxi took them to the Piazzale Roma, where Alessandro led her to a large, dark car. He loaded her luggage into the boot while Francine sank into the leather seat, an increasing sense of unreality beginning to creep over her. She still couldn't quite believe that she was actually married to this man. Every time she even thought about it, her chest would tighten until she had trouble breathing. Then the sun would reflect off the gold band on her finger, and she would *have* to believe it. The incredible had happened, and Alessandro Zancani really was her husband.

Alessandro got in beside her, and began to drive swiftly away. As they sped across the flat plain of the Veneto, the silence between them stretched on. He hadn't said a word to her since they had left Venice. Francine was very aware that it wasn't a comfortable silence. A raw tension seemed to be building between them, and her own nerves already felt so taut that she was afraid they might snap.

The plain began to give way to gentle hills, lit by the golden glow of the afternoon sun. The scene was very peaceful, but it didn't help to relax her in the least. She wished that Alessandro would say something—*anything*. Or that she could stop feeling so horribly tongue-tied with nerves, and could break the silence herself.

Alessandro eventually brought the car to a halt beside a villa set in the shelter of a hillside and flanked by tall, dark cypresses, like sentinels. An arched colonnade ran right along the front façade, with the doors and windows hidden in shadow behind it. A secretive place, Francine thought at once. And for the first time, she felt a deep surge of pure unease. No one knew that she was here. If she were to disappear, her family and friends wouldn't even know where to start looking for her.

She gave a quick, impatient shake of her head, and told herself she was being wildly fanciful. She wasn't going to disappear! All the same, her skin had grown a little cold, and it was with a strange reluctance that she followed Alessandro into the villa.

Inside, it was cool and shadowed. Tiled floors, pale walls and simple furnishings meant that it contrasted strongly with the opulence of the palazzo in Venice. Yet, Alessandro seemed as much at home in these surroundings as he did amid the magnificence of the palazzo.

It seemed to be unnervingly quiet inside the villa.

'Are we—are we alone?' Francine asked a little hesitantly.

'Of course,' Alessandro replied softly. 'The staff have all been sent away. I don't intend to share my honeymoon with anyone except you.'

His words should have excited her. The sense of unease just wouldn't go away, though. The dark tension between them was also still there, and Francine was sure that it was deepening. And becoming dangerous? she wondered, all of her nerves suddenly jumping.

Then she got very annoyed with herself. Why was she ruining what should have been the most marvellous day of her life by letting her imagination run out of control? What a stupid thing to do! She had to stop it right now.

As if to prove that she was worrying needlessly, Alessandro moved closer and lightly took her hand in his own.

'Come upstairs,' he invited softly.

The warmth of his touch immediately reassured her. It had just been her nerves playing games with her, she told herself with a silent sigh of relief. Everything had happened too fast; she hadn't had time to adjust.

He led her up the stairs, and then opened a door that led into a large bedroom with windows that looked out on to the gently curving, sunlit valley beyond. His fingers touched the soft silk of her dress, Francine felt the heat of his skin even through the fine material, and told herself that he had been tense because he had been waiting for this for too long.

But she had been waiting, as well. Waiting to hear the promised words of love.

'You said that, after the wedding, you'd tell me how you felt about me,' she softly reminded him.

'Yes, I did,' Alessandro agreed. 'But I think that I'll wait for just a little while longer,' he added in a voice that had grown so low and husky that she could barely hear what he was saying.

With one quick movement, he pulled her closer. Then he kissed her with a hard intensity which left both of them struggling for breath.

Francine was quite certain that he hadn't intended this to happen so soon—or so quickly—but she was secretly thrilled by the way that she could send her husband's desires rocketing out of control.

The room was so quiet that she could hear the gentle rasp of their bodies sliding together, frustrated by the layer of clothes that still separated them. Yet there was a pleasure in prolonging these moments, and delaying the intense pleasure of complete intimacy.

Alessandro's mouth began to move over her restlessly, and she knew that he wanted to feel her skin against his. He was increasingly impatient for the complete freedom of her body, still denied to him by the soft silk of her wedding dress.

He unfastened the lace covered bodice and slid it down to her waist, so that the softness of her breasts at last lay under his palms. Francine heard the light groan that sounded in his throat, a mixture of intense desire and relief. And the games that his lips and tongue were now playing with her made her gasp out loud, the pleasure was so delicious that it almost hurt. He circled the outer softness of her breasts with rings of kisses, spiralling inwards towards the aching tips, and then gently, oh so gently, catching them within his teeth, lightly nibbling until she really didn't think she could bear it any longer, she wanted the warmth of his mouth and the moistness of his tongue. And when he gave them to her, she thought she would faint with sheer delight, nothing in her entire life had ever been like this.

She wanted—ached—to tell him just how much she loved him. She realised that she had never told him, and then her mouth relaxed into a faint smile because there had hardly been time. This wasn't the right moment, though; she would wait until afterwards, when they were both lying at peace with each other.

There certainly wasn't any peace between them at the moment. Growing spasms of pleasure shot through her body as Alessandro relentlessly moved on in his journey of exploration. The dress was slid completely from her body, then his mouth trailed across her flat stomach, his hands circled her hips and forced her to remain still as his head moved still lower, his kisses left a devastating ache between the vulnerable tenderness of her inner thighs.

They were lying on the bed, now, with Alessandro swiftly and expertly removing the rest of their clothing. Her breathing, her whole world, seemed to have gone to pieces. Francine was desperate to touch him in return, she was amazed to find her hands moving over him with complete confidence, she revelled in the heat that burst from his skin, the powerful movements of his chest as his own breathing ran out of control, the convulsive jerk of his stomach muscles as she grew even bolder.

At the last moment, though, her new-found courage failed her.

Alessandro raised his head and looked down at her with blazing eyes. 'Don't stop!' he ordered roughly.

And so she touched him intimately for the first time. The hardness of his body awed and thrilled her, and gave her a strange sense of truly feminine power. As she gently caressed, she saw him grit his teeth and fight back the fresh waves of desire that swept over him, enjoying the pleasure and pain of prolonging these moments for as long as he could endure them.

Finally, though, he was forced to tear her hand away. He breathed very deeply a couple of times, somehow regaining a shadow of control.

'Such a clever girl,' he said thickly. 'But I thought that you would be.'

Before Francine had time to wonder what he meant by that, his own fingers slid back gently between her thighs, and suddenly she couldn't move, could only breathe in small gasps. This time, she didn't tense up, she simply gave way to the increasingly intense surges of pleasure, they washed through her faster and faster, until she seemed to be poised on a knife's edge.

'Do you like this?' Alessandro murmured in her ear.

She heard herself babble something incoherently as his mouth moved over her again, setting tiny fires burning beneath her skin wherever he touched her. Then her stomach knotted as his hands swept across it, in pursuit of fresh ways to torment her.

A mindless pleasure filled her, but still he held back, held back, torturing them both in the most exquisite way. His body beat against hers, massively aroused, and every muscle was rigidly tense with the effort of holding on to the last few strands of self-control, denying both of them the pleasure that they ached for.

Instead he stared down at her again, his gaze both fierce and triumphant.

'Are you going to want this—want me—for the rest of your life?' he demanded.

'Yes,' she cried softly. '*Yes*.'

That seemed to satisfy him. To her intense relief, he finally moved against her. Her body instantly became soft and receptive, so that there was no resistance as he slid inside her, and only the faintest sense of shock.

Then the pleasure began again, swift and frenzied, wave after wave, until Francine felt herself drowning in it. Darkness and light came together in an explosion of all the senses that left every one of her nerve-ends reeling. Down and down she tumbled, into a great chasm of dazzling sensations, clinging frantically to Alessandro who forced the pleasure to go on and on, past the point where she couldn't bear it any longer, until his own body shuddered convulsively and her entire world flew apart in one last starburst of exquisite delight.

Slowly, very, very slowly, she began the long drift back to reality. They both lay completely still, it was too much effort to move, almost too much effort to breathe.

Alessandro was the first to stir. He disengaged himself from her body, ignoring her small sound of protest. Then he propped himself up on his elbow, looking down at her, his eyes dark and burning.

In her innocence, Francine thought at first that he was beginning to want her again. Her own eyes briefly glowed; she was so totally head over heels in love that she was ready to give him absolutely anything. Her hands even began to move eagerly towards him, but then they became still as she saw the expression on his face more clearly.

His features were rigidly outlined in a way that she had never seen them before. Desire was certainly written there, but his mouth had set into a line that was hard and ruthless. But more terrifying than that was the clear contempt stamped on his face. Contempt, and something very close to hatred.

Francine shakily told herself that she was mistaken, she *had* to be mistaken. He couldn't possibly hate her. Not after what had just happened! Not when he still wanted her.

'Tell me something, my clever, beautiful Francine,' Alessandro said in a coldly controlled voice. 'Have you enjoyed your honeymoon?'

'You—you know that I have,' she said, her own voice suddenly fearful. At the same time, her eyes frantically searched his face for some sign that this was just a game, not to be taken seriously, just a game, *please*.

'Yes, I thought so. In fact, the whole thing's been quite an adventure, hasn't it? A new experience. And you're a girl who likes new experiences, aren't you?' he said, and she flinched at the deliberately caustic words.

'I don't know what you mean,' she whispered.

'I think that you do.' His face became frighteningly hard. 'But the fun's over now. I've accomplished everything that I set out to achieve. And I'm glad that you enjoyed your brief honeymoon, because, my dear wife, that is the last time that I shall ever touch you!'

After he had said those last cruel words, Francine felt as if he had actually hit her. She told herself that this had to be a nightmare. She must have fallen asleep, and now she was having an awful dream. If she could just wake herself up, everything would be all right.

But she had the terrible feeling that nothing was ever going to be all right again. And the really terrifying thing was that she didn't know *why* this was happening.

She dug her nails hard into her palms until it hurt so much that she knew she had to be awake. That was when the shock really hit her. For a few moments, she felt as if she couldn't even breathe. Then slowly, very slowly, she forced herself to face up to reality.

Alessandro was standing by the bed, now, looking down at her with that same dark mixture of desire and contempt. 'Nothing to say?' he challenged her, in a voice that suddenly seemed to belong to a stranger. His grey-green eyes locked on to her face, and for the very briefest of moments something flickered hotly in their depths. Then that iron self-control slammed back into place again, and they turned to pure ice. 'Later on, you'll probably want to know why this has happened,' he went on. 'Come and see me, and I'll tell you. In fact, it will give me a lot of pleasure to tell you. In the meantime, you may as well get dressed. Your body is enchanting, but I don't want it any more,' he finished with brutal finality.

Then he turned away from her and strode out of the room.

Francine had no idea how long she lay there, curled into a small, tight ball, keeping perfectly still, as if that would somehow ease the pain. Her eyes were closed so very tightly that her head began to ache. And when she did at last manage to move, to open her eyes again, she felt very stiff, very old, and completely exhausted, as if the sheer shock of what had happened had drained all her physical strength.

But why, why, *why* had he done it? That question kept hammering inside her throbbing head until she thought that it would drive her a little mad.

She had never done anything to hurt him, all she had done was fall in love with him. It made no sense for him to do this to her.

The only thing that was keeping her a little sane was the certainty that not all of it had been a complete sham. Despite all the terrible things he had said to her, he *had* wanted her. She might be miles behind him in experience, but even she could recognise the unstoppable force of genuine desire. She was quite certain that he had had to force himself to walk away from her. But it was possible to want someone and still hate them, wasn't it?

Very shakily, Francine pulled herself off the bed. She didn't want to put the cream silk dress back on—she wasn't even sure that she could bear the touch of it against her skin—but she had nothing else to wear. Her luggage was still downstairs. With a small shudder, she finally made herself put it on, and flinched as she felt the silk touch her skin, which was clammily cold from shock.

She left her hair loose and tangled around her shoulders, and she didn't dare even glance in a mirror. She was frightened of what she might see written on her face.

Now for the very hardest part of all. She had to go and find Alessandro, and demand to know why he had done this to her.

Francine didn't want to leave the room. What she really wanted was to be miraculously transported back to England, to her own small flat, where she could bury herself among her own personal possessions for some kind of comfort. She couldn't go anywhere, do anything, even start to think about living, though, until she learnt the truth about her marriage. She really would go quite mad if she had to spend the rest of her life wondering why Alessandro had done this to her.

When she finally found enough strength to open the door, the rest of the villa was totally silent, as if deserted. Francine knew that Alessandro was still here, though. Her heightened senses could pick up his presence, even though he was out of sight.

She took a couple of deep, steadying breaths, and slowly went down the stairs. Outside, it was a golden, perfect evening. It should have complemented the perfect first night of her marriage. That was obviously all a mockery, though, and Francine found herself suddenly hating the beauty of her surroundings.

She knew instinctively which room Alessandro was in. The spacious drawing-room, with wide windows that opened on to the terrace at the back of the villa. Beyond the formal gardens, the hills shimmered in the heat of late evening, and soft shadows crept across the valley as the huge red-gold sun sank even lower.

Alessandro was sitting in a chair, his gaze fixed on the doorway, obviously waiting for her. The very sight of him sent every small part of her spinning into turmoil. She vividly remembered *exactly* how it had felt when he had touched her. She couldn't believe that she was never going to be allowed to feel any of those things again.

'So,' Alessandro said in a rigidly controlled voice, 'you really do want to know why we've been through this little charade?'

'Of course I want to know,' she said, her own voice as brittle as glass. 'I don't believe that even you would do this kind of thing simply for fun!'

'Oh, no, not for fun,' Alessandro agreed, his tone immediately becoming grimmer. 'Tell me something, Francine. Have you spoken to your father lately?'

'My father?' she echoed in confusion. 'No, I haven't. You know I haven't. I remember telling you that he's filming in South America.' She shook her head, as if trying to clear it. 'Are you saying that my father has something to do with all of this?'

'He has everything to do with it. It's because of your father that I arranged to meet you. Because of your father that you're now married to me.'

Francine felt her mind begin to spin. 'But—you don't know my father. When I first told you about him, you said that you'd never even heard of him.'

'That was a lie,' Alessandro said coolly. 'Would you like me to apologise for it?' he added with some derision.

'I don't want you to do anything except explain what's going on here,' she said with a sudden rush of fierceness. 'And what do you mean, you arranged to meet me? We met by chance!'

'Of course we didn't. Absolutely nothing that has happened between us has been by chance.'

Francine abruptly sat down in the nearest chair. She was finding it almost impossible to take all of this in.

'You knew I was coming to Venice?' she managed to say at last.

'Of course. The calendar that your boss, Pete Drummond, came to Venice to shoot? It was for one of my subsidiary companies. I made sure that he knew about the job, and when he tendered for it—as I knew he would—I ensured that he was the successful applicant. I expected you to come with him as his assistant, not his model, but it didn't actually make any difference.'

Francine was totally stunned by this latest revelation. 'Those two men on the bridge,' she said slowly, but with growing anger, 'the two men who threatened me—did you arrange that, as well?'

'No, that was pure luck. I didn't leave the palazzo that night because of an urgent business call, as I told everyone. I'd phoned the airport earlier and found out that your plane had been delayed, so I walked down to the San Marco landing stage, to make sure that you had actually arrived. When I saw you get off the *vaporetto*, I followed you at a safe distance. I soon realised that you were getting lost in the back streets, and I was about to step in and help. I thought that would give me the perfect opportunity to introduce myself. Then those two thugs turned up, and that gave me the chance to make an even better first impression. The rest was easy. Much easier than I had expected.'

Francine fought furiously against the flush that was spreading right across her face. She, too, couldn't help remembering just how easy she had made it for him.

She took refuge in a fresh burst of anger. 'I still don't see what any of this has to do with my father!'

Alessandro's face instantly darkened, and she found the icy bleakness that turned his eyes stone grey quite terrifying.

'Paul James,' he said, 'your father, has ruined the life of my sister. That gives me every right to ruin his life in return.'

'My father doesn't even *know* your sister.'

'Oh, yes, he knows her,' Alessandro said in a voice that was very soft and yet very dangerous. 'He met her at a party, lured her to his home and seduced her. He's nearly fifty years old, and my sister's barely twenty, and she was completely innocent until she met him.' His eyes suddenly blazed with vivid anger. 'Don't you think that's something that deserves to be punished, Francine?'

CHAPTER SIX

FRANCINE just stared at her husband. Everything that he said only seemed to be confusing her more and more.

'You've never asked any questions about my sister, have you?' Alessandro said in a hard voice. 'You've worn her clothes, but you've never even asked her name.'

Francine wanted to blurt out that she hadn't been able to think of anything except *him*. It had been like that ever since she had first met him. She said nothing, though. This wasn't the time for such a confession.

'Giulia,' Alessandro went on. 'That's her name. She's just twenty, and very beautiful. She's been living in America for the past few months, because she had some nonsensical idea in her head about becoming a film star. I couldn't talk her out of it, so I decided to let her go ahead, and find out for herself just how difficult it is to get even a minor role. I've an aunt and some cousins living in Los Angeles, and I thought she would be safe if she stayed with them. To be sure, though, I flew out and visited her every so often. A few weeks ago, I went on such a visit and found my aunt almost hysterical because Giulia hadn't been home for two nights, and she didn't even know where to begin looking for her. I guessed that she'd been mixing with people from the film industry. I began calling in favours, used what influence I have to get answers to my questions. I finally learnt that Giulia had last been seen at a party in Hollywood—and she had left with Paul James.'

'My father,' Francine whispered. 'Then he really has met her.'

'But he wasn't content with just meeting her,' Alessandro said in a totally grim tone. 'I went directly to his house, and found Giulia in his bed! As soon as she saw me, she ran into my arms and burst into tears. It didn't take long to get the full story out of her. She had drunk rather too much at the party—Giulia isn't used to alcohol—and she naïvely believed Paul James when he said he wanted to be her friend, and help her career.' His mouth was rigid with anger. 'He helped her by taking her back to his house and seducing her!'

'My father would *never* do anything like that!' Francine protested in horror.

'Of course he would. He has no morals, no scruples. He used all his considerable experience with women to persuade my sister into his bed, and made sure that she enjoyed it so much that she wanted to stay there.' The disgust and fury in his voice deepened still further. 'He's nearly thirty years older than Giulia! He must have known how innocent she was—but it didn't mean a damn thing to him.'

'What did you do?' she found herself whispering.

Alessandro gave a smile so cold that she actually shivered. 'With difficulty, I stopped myself from killing him. Why spend the rest of my life in prison for someone as worthless as your father? And I remembered my own father's words—physical violence is the weapon of the stupid man. There are far more effective ways of taking revenge. I talked to people, discovered all I could about Paul James—and his weaknesses. I learnt about his vanity, and his true age, which he so carefully keeps a secret. And I discovered that he was about to begin work on a film which could have been the most important of his career. It would have taken him into the top league if it had been completed, and successful. It was the kind of role that would earn an Oscar nomination.'

'Yes, I know,' Francine said in a low voice. 'He was desperate to do that film, he said it was the role he had been waiting for all his life. He was completely devastated when it was cancelled at the very last minute.' Then her eyes suddenly flew wide open. 'You?' she said in disbelief. 'You did that?'

'Yes,' Alessandro confirmed, with grim satisfaction. 'I've many business and financial connections in America, and a great deal of influence. I managed to persuade some very important people that the film would be a financial disaster. They listened to me, and then withdrew their backing. Your father is now working on a second-rate film in the kind of lightweight role he hates. The film will almost certainly flop, and his reputation will nosedive with it.'

'You're so ruthless,' she said in a choked voice.

'I believe in revenge,' he said relentlessly. 'But ruining your father's career wasn't enough. It wasn't a personal blow.'

Francine raised her head and stared at him in sudden comprehension. 'So you decided to hurt my father through *me*, didn't you?' she said slowly.

'I looked for your father's biggest weakness, and found it was his daughter,' Alessandro agreed. 'He doesn't see you very often, but he does love you. So I decided to take you away from him.' A gleam of triumph began to show in his eyes. 'Your father knows that I was responsible for that film being cancelled, for him losing the best role of his career, and he hates me for it. I'm the very last person on this earth that he would want to see his beloved daughter married to.'

'And didn't *I* matter at all, in all these grand plans of yours for revenge?' she said hotly.

Alessandro merely shrugged. 'I knew there was no danger of you being truly hurt. Rather fittingly, Giulia herself convinced me of that. Your father talked to Giulia about you, and she passed on a lot of very useful information about your personal life. I know all about the men that you meet when you're working abroad in exotic locations, the casual affairs, the free and easy lifestyle. You're not a little innocent, Francine, no matter how much you might enjoy acting it at times. Your pride might have taken a knock, but this marriage was only ever one more adventure to you.'

Francine gave a small gasp. Oh, God, all those stories she had told her father, trying to pretend that she had the kind of lifestyle that matched his! Trying not to sound boring and ordinary. And she had succeeded only too well! Her father had certainly believed her, and now Alessandro did, too.

'You're Paul James's daughter in just about every way,' Alessandro went on, looking at her with clear disgust. 'In your lifestyle and your morals. If you'd been an ordinary, decent girl, then of course I'd never have touched you. The risk of genuinely hurting you would have been far too great.'

'You think I haven't been hurt?' she said incredulously.

'Oh, I'm sure that you're devastated at the thought of losing a wealthy and influential husband,' he said dismissively. 'But has any of this really touched you in any way? No, Francine,' he said with complete certainty.

'What if you're completely wrong about me?' she said in a choked voice. 'What if all those stories about my lifestyle weren't even true?'

For just an instant, Alessandro's face altered. Then his features darkened again, and his voice was hard when he answered her.

'Of course they're true. You proved that on the night I first brought you back to the palazzo. Just a couple of hours after meeting me, you found your way into my bed!'

That was the point when Francine finally gave up. He hadn't believed at the time that that had been a genuine mistake, and he certainly wasn't going to believe it now. Just as he would never believe that she loved him. She remembered that she had never said the actual words to him, and was suddenly glad. Let him go on thinking that she had married him because of who he was, a very wealthy and powerful man.

'So, what happens now?' she said in an utterly defeated voice.

Alessandro shrugged. 'That's up to you. I've already achieved everything that I wanted. I've made sure that you're married to the one man your father hates—and fears—more than anyone. And I've also made sure that the marriage is completely legal,' he added, his eyes briefly glittering. 'There's no question of an annulment.' Ignoring the sudden bright flush that his words brought to her face, he went on, 'Your father will very soon be aware that you've shared my bed. That, legally, you belong to me. It's a small punishment for what he did to my sister, but at least some part of our family honour will have been redeemed.'

Francine looked at him with drained tiredness. 'You're not just scarred on your face,' she said quietly, at last. 'I think that you're also scarred inside, where no one can see. You must be damaged, Alessandro, or you couldn't have done something like this.'

Then she turned away from him and quickly left the room, because she could feel the hot pressure of tears behind her eyes, and she was absolutely determined not to cry in front of him.

Later that evening, after darkness had fallen, Francine heard Alessandro leave the villa. She thought that he was probably returning to Venice. After all, there was nothing to keep him here—except a wife that he didn't want, she told herself with some bitterness.

The tears had long ago dried up, and now she walked around restlessly, quite unable to sit still even though she felt quite exhausted. She desperatedly wanted to speak to her father, to find out if any of Alessandro's incredible accusations against him were true, but that was impossible. He was still on that remote location in South America, and out of touch.

Francine just couldn't believe that her father would deliberately set out to seduce a naïve, twenty-year-old girl. There had to have been some mistake, some mix up!

But Alessandro had been so very certain. And would he have gone to such extreme lengths to get his revenge, if it weren't true?

She felt so utterly confused, she just didn't know who to believe. Her adored father, or her husband. There was one thing she was absolutely certain of, though.

Alessandro had had no right to use her in the ruthless way that he had.

Francine could feel a hurt anger growing inside her. And a new determination. She wasn't the kind of girl who let herself be used by anyone!

Ever since that devastating revelation, all she had wanted to do was run away somewhere very quiet and very familiar, where she could lick her deep wounds in private. She was suddenly beginning to feel differently, though. When Alessandro had walked out this evening, he must have thought that was the end of the affair—and the marriage. It certainly wasn't, though! she told herself forcefully, her eyes flashing brightly.

She had all night to make her plans. And in the morning, she would somehow find the strength of character to carry them through!

Since sleep was virtually impossible, Francine had plenty of time to think everything over very carefully. She did try to catnap for a couple of hours, but kept waking up shivering as she remembered the awful end to her wedding night.

She managed to force down some breakfast, even though the food kept threatening to stick in her tight, dry throat. Then she used the telephone and, in very slow English and just a handful of basic Italian words, finally managed to order a car to take her back to Venice. The fare would swallow up a large chunk of the money she had brought with her, but she didn't care. Money didn't seem in the least important right now.

By late morning, she and her luggage were on a *vaporetto* going back up the Grand Canal. She disembarked at the Piazza San Marco, picked up her cases, and walked steadily in the direction of the Palazzo Zancani. She was familiar with this part of Venice now; there was no danger of her getting lost. In just minutes, she was opening the door that led into the small, private courtyard garden at the back of the palazzo. Then, with a calmness that surprised even her, she pushed open the door to the palazzo itself, and went inside.

By the time she had carried her cases up to the first floor, she was out of breath and feeling the first small tremors of nervousness. Was she quite mad to come back here? she asked herself edgily. Too late to turn back now, though. Her decision had been made.

Then the door to the drawing-room opened and Alessandro came out. When he saw her, he stopped dead, and his face registered surprise and a dark displeasure.

'I thought that you would go running straight home to daddy,' he growled.

'Why should I?' she said, far more calmly than she felt. Her stomach was churning wildly, now! 'I'm an adult. I don't need someone to hold my hand when things go wrong.'

His grey-green eyes fixed on her face. 'Why are you here?'

'I'd have thought that was obvious. The vows that I took yesterday meant something to me, even though they clearly didn't to you. I'm not going to run out on my marriage!'

'In other words, you don't want to give up your position as Alessandro Zancani's wife,' he said in contempt. 'You want the money, the power, the position.'

I want you to *love* me! she nearly screamed at him. But she bit back the words; that was asking for the impossible.

'I think that I'm entitled to some compensation for the way that I've been used,' she said, holding her head very high and straight, and hoping he couldn't see the rigid tension in her shoulders.

'What are you suggesting? A marriage where we lead separate lives?'

'I'm not suggesting anything,' Francine said tautly. 'I'm *telling* you that I'm your wife. I'm also telling you that I intend to stay married to you!'

Alessandro's eyes instantly darkened. 'No one dictates to me!'

'You mean that no one's ever dared to—until now,' she retorted, throwing caution to the winds. 'But I dare, Alessandro. And I think that you've got to give me exactly what I want.'

'Why?' he challenged her fiercely.

'Because of your famous sense of honour. It doesn't matter what kind of reputation you think I've got. It still didn't give you the right to drag me into your dispute with my father. What you did was wrong. You owe me, Alessandro. And I'm calling in the debt.'

Francine was absolutely amazed that she had found the courage to confront him like this. Even now, she didn't really expect to win. Then she realised that Alessandro was picking up her suitcases.

'What are you doing?' she asked warily.

'Taking your bags to your room, of course.' He gave her the coldest smile she had ever seen. 'Don't gloat. You haven't won. I've simply decided that it would suit me very well to continue with this marriage for a while longer. Every day that you stay with me will cause your father more pain. And that was the object of this exercise, wasn't it?'

Francine stood very still. She hadn't even thought of that. She realised that she was being forced to choose between her father and her husband.

I have to stay with Alessandro, she told herself with a huge pang of conscience. I *have* to. I love him too much, I can't leave him. I just hope that Dad will understand one day.

Alessandro led her up the stairs to the bedroom she had been given on that very first night at the palazzo. Then he turned to her, his eyes locking on to her own with glittering intensity.

'I assume that you're not demanding that we share the same bed?'

There was a mocking note in his voice, and Francine immediately responded to it.

'We'll never sleep together again unless you ask—no, unless you *beg* me,' she retorted.

'I've never begged a woman—or man—for anything, so this will obviously be a marriage of convenience from now on.' A hot light briefly shone in his eyes, though, and Francine quivered slightly as she felt an answering pool of heat deep in the pit of her stomach.

For a few moments they simply stood and stared at each other, as if bound by something over which neither of them had any control. Then Alessandro growled something under his breath, turned abruptly away, and strode off.

Francine went slowly into the room, but didn't even have the energy to unpack. It was hard enough just standing upright on legs that now felt completely wobbly. She tottered over to the bed and collapsed weakly on to it. Now that Alessandro had gone, she could at last abandon the pretence of being strong and determined.

The next few days turned out to be the most difficult of her life. When Alessandro was actually at the palazzo he was distant and withdrawn. On the few occasions he spoke to her, his voice was remote, as if she were an employee, not his wife. There were just the two of them in the palazzo, no sign of any staff, and Francine remembered he had told her that he had given them all some time off. She longed for someone to talk to; someone to break the long, long silences and the emptiness that seemed to surround her. She was completely unhappy, but she didn't leave.

Then slowly, very slowly, things began to change. Alessandro began to join her for the evening meal, which Francine would spend the afternoon cooking, after hunting through the shops and markets for exotic ingredients. She loved trying out new recipes, and the kitchen in the Palazzo Zancani was a cook's dream. Although they never talked about personal matters, he would discuss other subjects with her, and even tell her about some of his current business projects. Francine was trying to learn Italian; she had been out and bought books and tapes. She tried out some of her carefully learnt phrases on Alessandro, and almost made him smile with her atrocious mispronounciation. With unexpected patience, he corrected her, and spent part of the evening speaking to her entirely in Italian, helping her to get a feel for the sound and structure of the language.

She adored being with him, loved listening to the dark tones of his voice. She told herself over and over that it would be so much easier if she could just fall out of love with him, but she knew that it wasn't going to happen. And all the time she longed for him to touch her, ached to touch him in return. It was so hard to stand close to him and have to keep her hands clenched by her side.

Sometimes, she would catch an unguarded glint in his own eyes, or sense a rigid tension in his body. That iron self-control would soon slam back into place, though, and she knew that even if he felt a trace of that fierce desire he had shown on their wedding night, he would never admit its existence.

At the end of the second week, Alessandro casually mentioned that Angelina would be returning the following day.

'Where has she been?' Francine asked.

'South, to visit relatives in Rome and Sorrento. She always takes a couple of weeks off in the summer to spend time with her family.'

'Isn't she married?'

'She's a widow. But she's got two sons and a daughter, and a handful of grandchildren.'

There was an odd note of envy in Alessandro's voice, something which Francine had never heard before. She looked up at him curiously, but he must have realised that he had revealed something he had never meant her to hear, and quickly changed the subject.

'You'll have to reach some kind of agreement with Angelina about the running of the house,' he said briskly. 'Until now, she's always had a free hand, and been solely responsible for hiring and firing staff.'

'I don't want to upset her or cause problems,' Francine said hurriedly. 'And although I like cooking, I'm not in the least domesticated in any other way. I'd like things to carry on just the way they are.'

Her answer seemed to satisfy Alessandro, and he left soon after that to work on some business papers in his study.

When Angelina returned late the following afternoon, the palazzo suddenly seemed to become alive. She bounced through the door and immediately threw her arms around Francine, giving her such an enormous hug that Francine could hardly breathe. A great flood of Italian poured out of her, so fast that Francine couldn't catch a single word. Then she switched to English.

'Such a surprise! And a *nice* surprise. That first night you came here, I knew you were the right one for Signor Zancani. I just didn't think he would have the sense to see it! But I'm very angry that I missed the wedding,' she scolded gently.

'Everyone missed the wedding,' Francine said wryly. 'There were only the two of us, and a couple of witnesses.'

'So romantic,' Angelina sighed. 'You must tell me all about it.'

'Oh—perhaps later,' Francine said evasively. Her wedding was a subject that her nerves were still too raw to discuss.

With Angelina back, the palazzo was suddenly far more busy. Part-time girls appeared to clean the magnificent rooms from top to bottom, tradesmen called, a gardener came to clear the weeds from the courtyard and plant fresh flowers, the windows were polished until they were crystal-clear.

Francine found herself missing the time that she had spent alone with Alessandro. There had been small moments of intimacy which she had treasured, and even cooking for him had been a secret pleasure.

Now that Angelina had taken over the kitchen again, Francine's days were completely free. She spent them exploring Venice, wandering slowly around the city, discovering something new every day. She visited churches and art galleries, travelled the canals on the *vaporetti*, went to bustling Murano with its famous glass works, and the green, peaceful island of Torcello.

The weather was hot and glorious, the city was jam-packed with people, yet there were still times when, without any warning, Francine would suddenly feel very cold and lonely. The chill seemed to be somewhere deep inside her, where the sun could never reach, and the sense of loneliness was something quite new to her. She had been independent and lived on her own for some time, but she had never *felt* lonely before. That had only started with her empty marriage. There were other days when she felt slightly sick, didn't want to eat. And she never slept well.

She knew that her looks should have mirrored her secret unhappiness and yet, perversely, they didn't. Her skin turned pale gold in the sun, and glowed. Her green eyes were bright and clear, and her hair shone with a new lustre, picking up amber highlights in the strong sunshine, every strand vividly coloured as it curled and danced around her shoulders.

Her life seemed to be settling into its new, strange pattern. The only small disturbance came a few days after Angelina had returned. Alessandro's housekeeper had been looking at her curiously for the last couple of days, and finally couldn't hold her tongue any longer.

'I don't understand,' she said bluntly to Francine, as they sat in the kitchen one afternoon drinking coffee. 'I know that modern marriages can be very different from the old fashioned kind, but I don't think it matters what kind of marriage you have, a husband and wife should still share a bedroom.'

The blunt statement made Francine jump, and then turn bright red. Then she jumped again as she heard Alessandro's voice behind her. He must have silently come into the kitchen just in time to hear that last remark.

'Angelina,' he said in an unexpectedly hard voice, 'are you interfering in something that's none of your business?'

'I organise the laundry, I can't help noticing that I'm washing the sheets from two different beds,' she said defensively.

'I'm a restless sleeper. I use a separate room so that I don't disturb Francine,' Alessandro said curtly.

Francine wanted to blurt out that she longed to be disturbed; that she lay awake half the night hoping—*aching*—to hear the sound of his footsteps outside her door. She didn't dare say anything in front of Angelina, though. In fact, she wouldn't have had the courage to say it to Alessandro even if they had been alone.

Angelina took notice of the look on Alessandro's face, and was wise enough not to ask any more questions. There was a light frown on her face for the rest of the day, though, and she obviously didn't like the idea that her employer's marriage might not be perfect.

Several days later, at the end of the evening meal, Alessandro raised his head and looked at Francine. 'Angelina reminded me that next weekend it will be the date that the original Zancani came to Venice, to make his fortune and build this palazzo. Traditionally, there's always a party here on that day to celebrate the founding of the Zancani family. Angelina tells me it would also be the ideal time to introduce my wife to Venetian society.'

'But—you can't want to do that,' Francine said warily. 'I mean—it isn't as if I'm—well, your proper wife,' she finished awkwardly.

'Oh, but you are,' he said softly. 'Our marriage is perfectly legal, in every way. And I do want you at that party. There has already been a great deal of rumour and speculation about you. People are beginning to wonder why I've kept you hidden away for so long.' He smiled unexpectedly. 'I want everyone to see that I haven't married someone with two heads or three legs!'

'I don't have anything to wear,' she protested feebly. 'And I'm *not* borrowing any more of Giulia's dresses,' she added with a sudden spark of defiance.

The mention of Giulia's name brought a swift darkness to his face, and Francine could have kicked herself. Why, oh, *why* had she had to mention his sister? Now he would begin to brood over the reasons for their marriage, and the evening would end in disaster.

The shadows lifted from his face more quickly than she had expected, though, and when he next spoke to her, his voice was terse but not cold.

'Venice is full of fashion shops. Buy whatever you need, and tell them to send the bill to me.'

'I can buy my own clothes,' she said at once.

'You can't afford the kind of dress you'll need for a party like this,' Alessandro said bluntly. 'As my wife, you'll be expected to wear something quite exclusive.' Then he added drily, 'For most women, spending a lot of money on clothes wouldn't be a problem.'

Francine gave a wry smile. 'I suppose I haven't had a lot of practice. When I'm working, I usually live in jeans and sweatshirts. I'll try and find something suitable for the party, though. And I'll let you pay for it—but only this once,' she warned.

Alessandro was clearly surprised by her attitude. He had obviously expected her to take full advantage of his offer, seizing the opportunity to buy herself a complete new wardrobe. He looked at her very thoughtfully for a few more moments and then, to her relief, changed the subject.

For the next couple of days, Francine spent some very pleasurable hours browsing through some of the most expensive fashion shops in Venice. Many of the dresses that she looked at were discreet and elegant, and very suitable. In the end, though, she murmured to herself, 'What the hell, let's knock-em-dead!' and chose one in a brilliant, exotic print. It clung sensually to her tall, supple body, and her hair clashed sensationally with the vivid swirls of deep emerald, darkest purple and smouldering pink.

Francine felt a growing mixture of nervousness and excitement as the night of the party drew nearer. Fresh flowers filled the palazzo with heady scents, the caterers were busy in the kitchen under Angelina's strict supervision, a small army of cleaners had polished absolutely everything to a rich, gleaming shine, and a live orchestra was rehearsing in the state room.

She went up to her room to get ready, and knew that there was another reason for the excitement building in the pit of her stomach. The last time there had been a party like this at the palazzo—the night she had met

Alessandro for the very first time—she had ended up in his bed! What if the same thing happened tonight?

Francine told herself over and over that it wouldn't happen. Alessandro had made it very clear that there would be no more intimate contact between them. But that didn't stop the small tremors that ran right through her.

It was a golden evening, with the sinking sun drenching the city with its last brilliant rays. Heat still hung heavily in the air and shimmered over the Grand Canal; people looked slightly flushed and moisture glimmered on their skin. Venice tonight was at its most hot and sensual, and Francine was aware of an answering glow in her own body.

She had showered earlier and washed her hair, leaving it to dry in a glistening mass of red-gold curls. It was time now to take the dress from the wardrobe and slip it on. Then she carefully applied make-up, slightly more than she usually wore, so that her green eyes seemed even bigger, her cheekbones shone softly with colour, and her lips looked full and moist. Tonight, she was going to make her first official appearance as Alessandro's wife, and she wanted him to be proud of her.

Her legs shook a little when she finally went downstairs, but her shoulders were straight and she held her head very high. The doors to the state room stood wide open, ready for the arrival of the first guests. There were no candles tonight, it was too hot. Instead, the state room was illuminated by the great chandeliers that hung in cascades of glittering crystal from the ornately painted ceiling.

Alessandro was already inside, and her heart thumped away at breakneck speed as she walked towards him. When she was still a few yards away, he turned and saw her.

His gaze raked over her from head to foot, taking in her flame bright hair, the fine bones of her face and unexpectedly full mouth, the generous lines of her body in the exotic dress. His face slowly changed and hardened, and his mouth set into a rigid line.

'Quite sensational,' he said tersely.

Francine bit her lip. 'You don't like the dress?' She had been so sure that he would. She had only bought it because she had been certain the vivid colours would draw his attention.

'Oh, yes, I like it,' Alessandro told her grimly. 'Every single man in this room tonight will like it. But it also reminds me of something I've been in danger of forgetting lately. That you're Paul James's daughter! That's exactly the kind of outfit that the daughter of such a man would wear.'

She told herself that she *wouldn't* cry, and instead took refuge in anger.

'What did you want me to wear?' she demanded. 'Something dull and dowdy? Are you so ashamed of me that you don't want anyone to notice me?'

Alessandro growled something under his breath that she couldn't hear. Then he turned round and strode off, leaving her standing in the centre of the state room feeling utterly miserable.

He brushed swiftly past Angelina, who was just coming into the state room to check that everything was ready. She glanced at her employer's black face in surprise, then walked towards Francine.

'You look beautiful!' she said with a huge smile. 'Every man in this room tonight will envy Signor Zancani.'

'He doesn't like my dress,' Francine said, biting her lip. 'He doesn't like anything about the way I look tonight. I don't think I even want to go to this party,' she finished, blinking hard to stop the tears falling.

'Of course you do,' Angelina said at once. 'And I think that he likes your dress very much. But he's also jealous; he only wants you to look this beautiful for *him*.'

'Jealous?' Francine echoed, in astonishment.

'Of course,' Angelina said cheerfully. 'I've seen jealousy many times; I recognise it when I see it. Now, don't cry or your eyes will be red and blotched. Enjoy the party, even flirt a little, if you want to. Jealousy can be a good thing, if you don't let it go too far.'

Francine was absolutely convinced that Angelina had to be wrong. Alessandro couldn't possibly be jealous! But she suddenly felt very much more cheerful, and almost began to look forward to the party again.

When Alessandro rejoined her a few minutes later, he said nothing, although he kept shooting dark glances in her direction. He seemed mesmerised by her appearance, didn't seem to be able to take his eyes off her.

Then the first of the guests began to arrive, and he was forced to give them his attention. Francine was relieved because it was highly disturbing to be the centre of such intense scrutiny.

She recognised some of the names and faces from the first party at the palazzo, but many of the others were completely new to her. She was aware of the murmurs going on all around her, and knew that she was the main topic of conversation this evening. Everyone was interested in the woman who had succeeded in ensnaring the most eligible man in Venice.

With growing confidence, Francine moved among the guests, stopping and talking to small groups while she sipped champagne. She deftly fielded questions about her marriage or simply smiled and changed the subject.

Later in the evening, as the orchestra played, couples began to dance. Francine felt in need of a breather, and decided to slip outside for a few moments for a breath of fresh air. Just as she was about to leave the state room, though, she heard two women talking just outside.

'Not the type that I expected Alessandro to marry. In fact, I didn't think he was ever going to marry at all! But she is gorgeous.'

'Yes, she is,' agreed the second woman. 'And either very tolerant, or very naïve. I certainly wouldn't invite my husband's ex-mistress to a party to celebrate my marriage!'

Francine, who had been about to walk away, stopped dead.

'If looks could kill, then one glance from Gisella would send pretty little Francine crashing to the floor,' said the first woman. 'Gisella's trying hard to hide it tonight, but everyone knows that she's absolutely furious about losing Alessandro.'

'Perhaps she hasn't lost him,' said the second woman, with a sophisticated laugh. 'Maybe Alessandro thinks he can have a wife *and* a mistress.'

'Perhaps he already has them both,' suggested the first woman slyly. 'I have heard that he's spent an occasional evening away from home since his marriage.'

They both laughed at that, and Francine wanted to die with pure humiliation.

She quickly turned away and headed blindly back into the state room. She certainly didn't want to come face to face with either of those women.

She hadn't known Gisella was here tonight; she must have slipped in late, after all the other guests had arrived.

Francine remembered the older woman's perfect face, framed with that startling jet-black hair. And the experience in her eyes. The perfect partner for a worldly man like Alessandro.

It doesn't have to be true, she told herself, trying to control her erratic breathing. All right, so you don't have a proper marriage, but that doesn't mean Alessandro is—is——

Sleeping with that woman, she forced herself to finish, with a small shudder. She really couldn't bear even to think about it.

And where *was* Gisella? Francine still hadn't seen her. Perhaps those two women had made a mistake, she told herself with new hopefulness. They had just seen someone who looked like Gisella, and jumped to all the wrong conclusions.

Couples were moving slowly around the dance-floor in front of her, and Francine forced herself to focus on them. Forget you heard that conversation, she told herself. Forget that Gisella even exists.

She suddenly saw Alessandro's dark, distinctive head, and her heart gave a queer, missed beat. Then it almost stopped beating altogether because he was dancing with one of his guests. She was looking up at him and laughing, and her exquisite body was pressed intimately close to his.

The woman in his arms was Gisella.

CHAPTER SEVEN

A BLINDING anger filled Francine. Without even thinking what she was doing, she walked straight over to them and stared Gisella straight in the face.

'Excuse me,' she said in a very clear voice, 'I would like to dance with my husband.'

The black-haired older woman looked back at Francine with cool and calculating eyes, as if debating whether to challenge her directly or not. Then she obviously decided that this was not the right time or place. Instead, she looked up at Alessandro and gave him a brilliant smile.

'It looks as if I'll have to give you back to your new little wife—for a while.'

Then she gracefully retreated, leaving Francine face to face with her husband.

'What the hell do you think you're doing?' Alessandro growled at her in a low undertone.

'Reclaiming something that's mine—even if it is only temporarily,' she retorted. 'Now, are you going to dance with me before we attract any more attention?'

Alessandro glanced round and obviously realised that the small scene was arousing intense curiosity in the people around them. He pulled her towards him, and Francine fought hard to suppress a shiver of pure delight as she felt his arms go around her. She hadn't forgotten that other woman, though.

'What is Gisella doing here?' she demanded, amazed at her own boldness.

'She's a guest,' Alessandro said tautly.

'She's your ex-mistress!' Francine threw back at him accusingly. 'And I don't want to see her in this house ever again.'

'Don't ever tell me who I can or can't invite to my own house,' he warned softly.

'*Our* house,' she said hotly. 'At least, while we're still married.'

'Keep your voice down,' Alessandro ordered. 'I won't have this turned into a public quarrel.'

'You should have thought about that before you invited her here,' Francine retorted, still astonished that she was having the nerve to stand up to him like this. It was probably because she was so blazingly angry at seeing that woman in his arms. And jealous!

'You have to accept that there were other women in my life before I met you.'

'Oh, I'll accept that. But I won't accept that they're *still* in your life!'

'Gisella is a friend,' Alessandro said in a terse voice.

'A very close friend!'

She knew that her refusal to drop the subject was making his own temper rise dangerously, but she couldn't help it. She had *hated* seeing him dancing with Gisella, she wanted to push the beautiful, supercilious woman straight off the balcony into the Grand Canal!

'She's only interested in you because of who you are,' Francine rushed on, the words pouring out of her. 'Why can't you see that? You're Alessandro Zancani, ex-racing driver, ultra-successful businessman, owner of one of the most beautiful palazzos in Venice, very eligible and rich bachelor—at least, until you got involved with me. All those things make you quite irresistible to that kind of woman.'

'Oh, but I know that,' he agreed, his tone suddenly turning very harsh. 'After all, you've just listed all the reasons why *you* were so willing to fall into my bed!'

That certainly shut her up. In fact, it knocked the breath right out of her. Oh, God, he *still* believed she had only married him because of his status and the material things he could give her!

She danced on automatically, her body stiff against his, very aware of the answering tension in Alessandro's own body. The music slowed, became more soft and intimate, but neither of them relaxed a fraction. In fact, the tension between them deepened until it seemed to become almost visible. Francine could feel her nerve ends vibrating softly with the strain, any moment now they were going to snap completely——

Another couple circled past, and the man paused and smiled at them.

'Why don't you kiss your new bride, Alessandro?' he suggested with a smile.

Other guests took up the idea with enthusiasm, and Francine's heart lurched as she realised that her first kiss from Alessandro since her wedding day was going to have to be in front of all these people. And while he was still in a black, angry mood!

Alessandro also seemed to be fighting conflicting emotions. He must have realised, though, that he couldn't refuse to kiss his wife without triggering off a great wave of suspicion and rumour about his marriage. His face darkened, then showed an unexpected flush of colour. Then he pulled Francine closer.

'Just one kiss,' he ordered in a low voice that only she could hear. His eyes briefly blazed. 'I think that we should both be able to manage that.'

His lips closed over hers before she had the chance to reply, and Francine instantly forgot that she was standing in the middle of the magnificent state room in the Palazzo Zancani; forgot that dozens of exquisitely dressed people were standing around them, toasting their health and happiness as they kissed.

She was only aware of the hard warmth of his mouth, the fast thudding of his heart behind his powerful ribcage. She wanted the kiss to go on and on forever, but it didn't, couldn't, and she was dismayed to hear herself making a small, helpless sound of protest as he finally released her again.

Alessandro stared down at her for a few moments, his eyes lit by a small flame that slowly died as he regained control of himself.

Then he turned away, took a glass of champagne that someone was holding out to him, and held it up high.

'To my marriage,' he said, and Francine wondered if she was the only one who could hear the haunting note of mockery in his voice.

The rest of the evening seemed to pass in a dream. She knew that she was talking fairly coherently to people sometimes in English and sometimes in very halting Italian. She drew admiring glances from many of the men, and speculative looks from the women, who were clearly wondering how she had managed to catch the prize which had slid elusively through their own fingers. She stood at Alessandro's side as he circled among his guests. And all the time, she was aware of Gisella in the background, shadowing them, like a spectre at the feast.

Francine was relieved when the party finally came to an end, in the early hours of the morning. She felt totally exhausted. She murmured an excuse about a headache and slipped up to the silence and privacy of her own room before the last guests had left. For a while, she sat by the window, her hot forehead pressed to the coolness of the glass. Outside, the water of the Grand Canal glittered darkly, and people still wandered around in the soft heat of the night.

She let out a gentle sigh. What had she accomplished this evening? Nothing, she told herself. Except to alienate Alessandro even further! But what had she expected to accomplish? She didn't really know. But she had had vague dreams, unspoken hopes...

'Stupid, *stupid*,' Francine whispered under her breath. 'Did you really think a dazzling dress, a dance, even a kiss, would get you what you really want?'

The palazzo had fallen silent, now, the last guest had gone, the orchestra departed, and the clearing up would be left until the morning. In the silence, though, Francine heard the sound of distant footsteps. Footsteps that gradually came nearer.

She almost stopped breathing. Alessandro's, they had to be Alessandro's! No one else would come to her room. Had he forgiven her? Had that kiss reminded him irresistibly of the pleasure they had once shared?

Her eyes grew huge, her skin felt as if it were on fire. The footsteps were almost outside her door, now, and they were slowing down—stopping——

Then Francine heard the sound of a woman's voice, low laughter, a soft, sensual murmur. And, finally, silence, as if that voice had been stifled by a kiss.

She knew exactly how Alessandro's kisses could reduce a woman to silence.

The footsteps finally started up again, moving away from her door and fading into the distance. They were going in the direction of Alessandro's suite of rooms. Who was he taking to bed? Francine wondered with quite unbearable pain. It wasn't hard to guess. The beautiful Gisella!

She sat like a stone, utterly cold inside, the heat and humidity of the night no longer touching her in any way. Even the pain inside her seemed to creep through her body with icy fingers.

With a huge effort, she forced herself to her feet. You've fought her once tonight, she told herself. Do it again!

Walking like an automaton, she opened her door, went along the unlit corridor, made herself go in the direction of Alessandro's bedroom.

She actually got within a few yards of his door. Then she stopped. She just couldn't go any further. Her head was thumping and her heart ached with an almost physical pain. And she couldn't get rid of the awful, vivid pictures inside her head. Alessandro kissing that perfect mouth; Alessandro softly stroking that fine skin with his clever, experienced hands. And Alessandro finally moving towards her, his body deeply aroused——

Stop it! Francine told herself in sudden panic. Don't do this to yourself, or you're going to go quite mad!

She stood there, suddenly shivering violently. Part of her still stubbornly wanted to go on, see the very worst, but another part knew that she just couldn't bear to do it, to know for certain what was going on in Alessandro's room tonight. If she didn't have to look at it, perhaps she could even pretend it wasn't happening.

Very slowly, she turned away. It was pointless to go back to her room, there was no chance of her getting any sleep. Instead, she forced her shaking legs to take her downstairs, back to the huge state room.

As she went in, she switched on the lights, so that the great chandeliers blazed with glittering brightness. She didn't want to be in the dark. Darkness encouraged black thoughts, and there were already too many of them inside her head.

The state room was just as the guests had left it. The cleaners wouldn't be arriving until the morning, to clear away the debris of the party. Francine wandered among the empty champagne glasses, the plates of half-eaten food, the great bowls of flowers, drooping slightly now after the heat of the evening.

Eventually, she slumped into a chair set to one side of the great fireplace. There had been no fire tonight, of course. She almost wished there were, though, she still felt so chilled inside.

She had no idea how long she sat huddled in the chair. At last, though, a glimmer of light began to show outside the windows. The long, long night was almost over.

Francine stood up slowly and stretched her cramped limbs. Then she walked over to the nearest window and opened it. Fresh air brushed lightly against her face, carrying with it the faint tang of salt from the sea. Outside, the Grand Canal was uncharacteristically quiet. The night people had finally gone home, now that dawn was breaking, and the tourists that filled every hotel in Venice were either still in bed, or eating a very early breakfast before launching on another full day of sightseeing.

'There's something very special about Venice at dawn,' murmured Alessandro's voice from just behind her. 'The city's half asleep, half awake, like a satisfied lover trying to rouse herself to face another day.'

Francine's entire nervous system felt as if it had gone completely haywire. She hadn't heard him approach; she hadn't even known that he had come into the state room.

Her shattered nerves, and the raw memories of last night, made her strike back at him immediately.

'Of course, you'd know all about the way satisfied lovers behave, wouldn't you?' she said very bitterly.

Alessandro didn't reply at once, but it was a brittle, dangerous silence. Francine held her breath, terrified that he would retaliate with deliberate cruelty. What if he decided to tell her exactly what had happened last night? What he had done—and with whom? She knew she couldn't bear that, she didn't want to hear Gisella's name, *didn't want to hear it*.

When he finally spoke, though, his voice was low and controlled.

'Don't you think that I'm entitled to take a lover?'

'You're married!' she burst out.

He gave a cynical laugh. 'Men have been ignoring their marriage vows since the beginning of time. Why should I be any different?'

Because you've got a wife who loves you, she ached to say. That would be stupid, though. And he wouldn't even believe her.

'You're a Zancani,' she said at last, in a much duller tone. 'Your name obviously means a lot to you, so you shouldn't do anything to dishonour it.'

Surprise lit his grey-green eyes. He clearly hadn't been expecting her to say anything like that.

'Yes, I've got a wife,' he agreed softly. His hand closed around her arm, and her skin instantly burnt at his touch. 'But this has been a marriage where there have been a lot of empty nights.'

Francine stared down at his hand, saw its darkness against her own light golden skin, and briefly closed her eyes. Every time he touched her, she wanted to melt, it just wasn't fair that she should feel like this when none of the tumultuous feelings inside her were returned.

'It isn't my fault that your nights are empty,' she said in a tight, strained voice. 'Please let go of me.' If he didn't release her very soon, she was terrified that she might do something really crazy—like trying to touch him in return.

But Alessandro didn't seem to want to let go. The chandeliers inside the state room still bathed the room with light, competing with the glow of dawn from outside, so that she could see every feature on his face with absolute clarity. The scar on his cheek stood out with shocking starkness in the revealing light, his mouth was set into a hard but highly sensual line, and a bright heat was beginning to stir in the depths of his eyes, turning them to molten green.

His gaze stayed locked on to her own face, as if he couldn't force himself to look away.

'I never get tired of looking at you,' he said very abruptly, to her astonishment.

Francine swallowed hard. She certainly hadn't expected him to say anything like *that*. 'What—what do you mean?'

He raised his hand and let his index finger lightly trace the shape of her forehead, her brow; then he touched her mouth for just an instant.

'Such an unusual face,' he said softly. 'Not quite beautiful, but very unique. It would be a huge mistake to fall in love with you, because other women would always be second best, in comparison.'

'But that won't be a problem for you, will it?' she said very unsteadily. 'You don't love me—do you, Alessandro?'

She hadn't meant it to sound like a question, but that was the way it had come out, and it hung tensely in the air between them.

Then his face darkened. 'How could I love you?' he said almost harshly.

It wasn't the answer she had braced herself to hear. She had expected a blunt, cruel, 'No'.

Don't read anything into it, Francine warned herself quickly. Don't run the risk of being hurt all over again.

But there was such an odd light shining in Alessandro's eyes now, and his fingers were still holding on to her arm, as if he couldn't make himself let go.

Her heart began to pound so fast that she felt slightly dizzy. She swayed towards him, nearer and nearer, until she could feel the heat of his body radiating in fierce waves. Triumph surged through her as she realised that she might not be able to make him love her, but she could certainly make him *want* her.

As if to confirm that, his other hand rested against the faint swell of her stomach, then moved up across her ribs, finally pausing just below the swell of her soft breast. Her heart slammed against his palm, telling him more than she wanted him to know.

'We could so easily drive each other mad,' Alessandro muttered. 'Teasing, playing games, driving each other to the very limit.'

His thumb brushed against the underswell of her breast, and she instantly shuddered. Completely unable to help herself, her own hand slid inside the thin material of his shirt, so that she was touching his hot, smooth skin. His muscles immediately clenched under her fingertips, as if he were fighting his own reaction to her closeness. Then they slowly relaxed again, as if acknowledging the inevitable.

Alessandro murmured something in soft Italian that she didn't understand. She tried to pretend that they were words of love, although she knew that they couldn't be. Then his thumb moved again, provoking the hard tip of her breast into a cascade of utterly sensual sensations.

Francine closed her eyes, she didn't want those feelings ever to stop, didn't want *him* to stop. But Alessandro's hand became still again, as if he had suddenly realised what he was doing. His breathing was hard, his body tense, and his voice was harsh again when he spoke to her.

'I made a bad mistake when I decided to take my revenge on your father through you. It hasn't worked out at all the way I planned it. You're not the person I expected you to be. I'm not used to failure,' came his forced admission. 'And I don't like it. But I do like *this*——'

His hand moved against her again, with unbridled impatience this time, seeking out the soft, hot, intimate places of her body, then caressing them with an unexpected gentleness that tore down all her defences.

Don't give in, don't give in, you'll be sorry! Francine told herself a little frantically. But it was too late, she could already feel herself surrendering, she couldn't help it. The powerful surge of love was too strong.

As if immediately aware of her acquiescence, Alessandro swiftly swung her up into his arms. Then he carried her easily out of the state room and up the stairs. Francine's heart was thumping so loudly that she was sure it could be heard all over Venice, and where her body touched his, she was aware of his own pulses beating in a matching frantic rhythm.

They reached the door to his room and she clung on to him fiercely, terrified that he might change his mind. As if to reassure her, he bent his head and kissed her with hard intensity. Then he freed one hand, so that he could open the door.

Without any warning, Francine was hit by a sickeningly vivid wave of memory. At the same time, a shrill voice began to shriek inside her head. Stop, stop, *stop*. Just a few hours ago, he had been here with another woman! Did she want to share the same bed as his mistress?

She instantly felt sick. How could she bear even to go into the room, knowing that the other woman's perfume would still be lingering in the air? The scent of their shared pleasure would be on the very sheets of the bed?

She shivered deeply with revulsion. Then her fists began to pummel against Alessandro's chest. 'Let go of me,' she moaned. '*Put me down*!'

She felt the wave of shock that ran through him at her sudden attack. Then his face darkened. 'What the hell——?'

'How dare you?' she yelled at him, anger bursting out of her, fuelled by the sheer pain of what he was doing to her. 'So much for your famous sense of honour. You make my father look like a saint!'

Alessandro's eyes had grown as stormy as her own, deep grey and threatening.

'I don't know what this is all about, but let me give you a warning,' he said grimly. 'Don't ever again compare me to your father.'

'Why not?' she threw back at him. 'You accused him of having no morals, no sense of decency. Well, how do you describe *your* behaviour tonight?' She shook herself free of him. 'I'm getting out of here,' she said in a tormented voice. 'I can't take any more of your cruelty.'

'Cruelty?' Alessandro repeated incredulously. 'I've never hit you, never forced myself on you in any way.'

Her head shot up, sending her hair flying out in a cloud of brilliant colour. 'Do you think I'm talking about physical violence?'

'Then what else?' he demanded. 'What kind of cruelty am I supposed to have inflicted on you?'

Francine couldn't believe that he had actually said that. That, incredibly, he didn't seem to realise what this was all about.

'You're planning to take me into your bedroom and make love with me on the same bed that you've just shared with your mistress!' she accused, almost hysterically. 'If that isn't cruelty—mental cruelty—then I don't know what is!'

'My *mistress*?' he said, glaring at her. 'What the hell are you talking about?'

'Oh, of course, I forgot. Gisella is just a *friend*, isn't she?' Francine retaliated with deliberate sarcasm. Then she rounded on him with fresh anger. 'I heard the two of you last night,' she said fiercely. 'You even stopped outside my door, to make sure that I heard! Then you took Gisella to your bedroom.'

'I didn't go anywhere near my room last night,' Alessandro said in a tight voice. 'After the party was over and everyone had finally gone, I left the palazzo. I walked around the city for a couple of hours; I do that sometimes at night when I know I won't be able to sleep. I returned here just after dawn, and came straight to the state room, where I found you.'

Francine stared at him in stunned shock for a few moments. Then her eyes clouded over again. 'I don't believe you,' she said in a low voice.

'Look at me!' he ordered. 'I'm still wearing the same clothes as last night. I haven't been back to my room yet, to change them.'

Her gaze slowly slid back to him, and she saw he was telling the truth. He was wearing the same dark, beautifully cut suit, although the crisp white shirt was a little ruffled where she had undone the buttons and slid her hand inside, to touch his hot skin.

She licked her dry lips. Had she made a terrible mistake? And one which he would certainly never forgive?

'If it wasn't you, then—then who did I hear going to your room?' she asked apprehensively.

'A couple of guests who abused my hospitality, I should think,' Alessandro said tersely. 'They're probably still in there. Do you want to open the door and take a look?'

'No,' she whispered. 'And I'm sorry for what I said. Really sorry.' She knew that the words were quite inadequate, though. She swallowed very hard. Oh, *hell*, she had made a mess of this.

Was there still a chance she could put it right? Somehow undo some of the damage? She knew that she had to try, because she might never get another chance.

'Do you think that we could—well, forget about all this?' she said falteringly.

'No.' His reply was harshly final, and left no room for compromise. 'Any relationship has to have an element of trust, even one like ours,' Alessandro went on, his face set into forbiddingly hard lines. 'I told you that Gisella was only a friend, but you chose not to believe me. You thought I was capable of sleeping with two different women in the same night. In the same bed! Perhaps you should stop judging people by your own low standards, Francine,' he said in contempt, his cutting words making her physically flinch.

'I do believe you,' she cried.

'It's no longer of any importance. The damage has been done. It's also reminded me of what you are really like, and it's certainly cured me of any desire I might have had to sleep with you. Goodnight, my dear wife,' he finished, the cynically spoken endearment bringing a sudden flood of tears to her eyes.

He didn't see them. By then, he had already turned away and strode off.

Francine felt very close to complete despair. She had said and done all the wrong things, and totally ruined the only chance she had had of some kind of reconciliation with Alessandro.

Yet, surely not *all* of it had been her fault? she said to herself miserably. She had made a genuine mistake, and Alessandro should have realised how devastated she had been by the thought of him sleeping with another woman. She knew that he would never admit that he had been wrong in any way, though, and her feet dragged tiredly as she very slowly went back to her empty, lonely room.

For the next few days, a very chilly atmosphere pervaded the entire palazzo. Alessandro spent little time at home, and Francine had to endure both his absence and Angelina's increasingly accusing glances. She was clearly beginning to realise that there was something very wrong with her employer's marriage, and obviously thought that Francine should pull herself together and do something about it.

As summer finally gave way to the early days of autumn, there was a very slight improvement in their relationship. Alessandro began to appear at evening meals again, and no longer seemed to be going out of his way to avoid her. There was still a great deal of tension between them, though, and Francine never felt relaxed when she was near him. Sometimes, she would tell herself that she had to talk to him about what had happened that night of the party, but she could never quite find the nerve. She was always terrified of making things even worse. For his part, he would often fix his grey-green gaze on her with such intensity that she would actually shake inside. His face would be dark and brooding at such times, and his body rigid with an inner anger. He clearly hadn't forgotten—or forgiven—and Francine sometimes despaired that he ever would.

She realised that her life seemed to have slid into an odd kind of limbo. She had cut off all her ties with her old life, but it was impossible to settle into her new one.

It was too uncertain, and the future was blurred. Sometimes, she found herself longing to be back in the studio with Pete, working flat out on some new and exciting project, her life furiously busy but uncomplicated. She couldn't go back, though; he had a new assistant now. He probably assumed she was blissfully happy with her new husband and had almost forgotten about him.

She filled her empty days with endless sightseeing. In Venice there was always something new to see, somewhere interesting to go. She knew that she couldn't go on like this indefinitely, though. She had to make some difficult decisions, and get her life back on some kind of meaningful course again. In the end, though, she always shied away from those decisions because they involved Alessandro. Perhaps even meant leaving him, if this relationship—or non-relationship—continued to go nowhere. And she wasn't ready to walk out because, damn it, she still loved him! She knew that his rejection of her should have cured her, but it hadn't. She didn't think that *anything* would, and the thought of loving him forever, without ever getting anything in return, was absolutely terrifying.

The weather was slightly cooler, now, and the crush of tourists beginning to ease just a little. Francine got up one morning and saw faint fingers of mist drifting over the canal. She knew that they would disappear with the first warmth of the sun, but it was the first real sign of autumn. She gave a huge sigh. She couldn't stay here all winter. But what else could she do? Where could she go?

She wished that she could go back to being the well-organised, determined and independent girl she had been at the beginning of summer. She didn't like this lethargic state she had drifted into, but she just couldn't seem to do anything about it.

After a long shower, she slowly dried herself and then reached into the wardrobe for a cotton skirt. It felt a little tight when she put it on, though, and so she tossed it to one side and reached for another.

A small puzzled frown crossed her face when she found that one didn't feel very comfortable, either. 'What has Angelina been doing with the laundry?' she wondered out loud.

She was quite sure she hadn't put on any weight. Her appetite hadn't been very good for the past couple of weeks, and she had eaten far less than usual.

When she glanced down at herself, though, she could see that her stomach wasn't quite as firm and flat as usual.

'You're out of condition,' she murmured. 'You'd better start taking some proper exercise before everything starts to sag!'

She reached into the wardrobe for a loose-fitting dress. Before she put it on, though, she stood in front of the full length mirror and looked at herself again.

She was wearing only a pair of lace-trimmed panties, and hadn't yet put on the matching bra. As she stared at her body, though, something about it disturbed her. It looked—different.

You're imagining it, Francine told herself uneasily. She reached for the bra, and hooked it up, and discovered that also felt tight. Her breasts, always full, now seemed to be straining at the thin material.

Suspicion began to creep through her, closely followed by the first stirrings of panic.

She fished her diary out of the drawer, turned the pages almost feverishly and checked dates. Then her eyes flew wide open. She hadn't had a period since a couple of weeks before her wedding!

She hadn't even thought about it. She was sometimes irregular, and anyway, there had been too many other things occupying her mind.

Her hand flew to her stomach, and she remembered all those times recently when she had felt faintly sick. She had put it down to stress and anxiety—but that didn't make your stomach and breasts swell!

Francine sat down on the edge of the bed very abruptly, her legs suddenly feeling totally weak. She was shocked, amazed, excited and disbelieving.

Could it have happened after making love just that once? she asked herself shakily. Yes, of course it could! She wasn't naïve, she knew it was perfectly possible to get pregnant the first time. And neither of them had taken any precautions. Of course, Alessandro believed she led a promiscuous lifestyle and had almost certainly assumed she was on the Pill. And Francine, head over heels in love with her husband, hadn't even given a thought to contraception. For those first few hours she had believed she had a blissfully happy marriage, she hadn't cared if she became pregnant, she had wanted half a dozen children with Alessandro.

Slow down, she warned herself. This could be a false alarm, you'll have to take some kind of test and make sure.

But, inside, she knew that she didn't need any test. She suddenly wanted to give a great yell of pure excitement, but stopped herself. This certainly wasn't a good time to have a baby, with her marriage in a mess and her own life drifting along aimlessly!

Francine realised that she didn't care, though. As far as she was concerned, this was the most marvellous thing that had ever happened to her.

'You're mad,' she told herself with a huge grin. 'Quite mad!'

Then she sat there for simply ages just gently cradling the very slight swell of her stomach, feeling quite awe-struck and deliriously happy.

She hugged her secret to herself all day. She longed to blurt it out to anyone, *everyone*, but forced herself to keep quiet. Alessandro had the right to be the first to know.

He'll be pleased, she told herself over and over. He *will* be pleased. She kept lapsing into this delicious fantasy where his face lit up at the news, he was delighted, overwhelmed, and everything miraculously became all right, as if a good fairy had waved a magic wand over their lives.

Francine knew that her eyes were overbright, she felt almost feverish with anticipation. When Alessandro joined her for dinner that evening, she wanted to blurt the news out straight away, but forced herself to wait for just the right moment.

She chattered away nervously all through the meal. His eyes seemed extra dark tonight, and his mouth was set in a forbiddingly tight line.

All that will change when I tell him, she comforted herself. She would wait until the very end of the meal, when he was relaxing with a glass of wine.

She felt the growing flush of excitement on her skin, and was sure that her eyes were quite brilliant. She didn't realise that she was licking her lips, turning them soft and moist, until she caught Alessandro staring fixedly at her mouth.

A few moments later, he raised his eyes to hers, and she realised they were a brilliant shade of green.

'You look different tonight,' he said softly.

Her heart jumped. He had noticed! And in just a few more minutes, she would tell him why she looked different.

'Tell me something,' he went on, in a voice that was still low and suddenly had a dangerous edge. 'How do you spend your days, Francine? What do you do during all those long hours when I'm not here?'

'I—I go sightseeing,' she said uncertainly, slightly unnerved by the unexpected question and his still darkening features.

'On your own?'

'Of course. I don't know anyone in Venice.'

'It doesn't take long to get to know someone. And you're very good at meeting people.'

She looked at him warily. 'What do you mean?'

Impatience and black anger abruptly crossed his face. 'Don't let's play games, Francine. You've got a certain look on your face, a look that I know only too well.'

'I'm just excited about something——' she began, but Alessandro didn't allow her to finish.

'Of course you are,' he said in a hard voice. 'Women always find a new lover exciting. You look as if you've just got out of bed, Francine. What I want to know is your lover's name!'

CHAPTER EIGHT

FRANCINE sat in totally stunned silence. His accusation had completely taken her breath away. Even if she could have thought of something to say, she wouldn't have been able to get the words out.

'Did you think I wouldn't find out?' Alessandro said harshly. 'I suppose you've done it to punish me. You still think that Gisella's my mistress, don't you? This is your way of getting your revenge. What's the next step?' he demanded, his eyes flaring darkly. 'To move in with him?'

Somehow, Francine found her voice. 'I haven't got a lover!' she said chokingly.

Disbelief was written all over Alessandro's face. 'You're a girl who likes good times and adventure. You sure as hell don't get either of those things in museums and art galleries!'

'Why do you always believe what other people say about me?' she burst out. 'Why can't you just look at me and see me the way I am?'

'But I can see you,' he growled. 'I can see the light in your eyes and the colour in your face. You haven't looked like that since our wedding night!'

Those last words seemed to have been dragged out of him with huge reluctance. Francine realised that, incredibly, he was behaving like a man who was almost uncontrollably *jealous*.

But he can't be, she told herself, her heart suddenly pounding. He was probably only concerned that she would involve his family name in some kind of scandal. Or that she would make him look a fool, because no one would ever expect Alessandro Zancani's wife to take a lover.

'Our marriage was the first big mistake I've ever made in my life,' he said grimly. 'I should never have got involved with you.'

'Not your first mistake,' Francine said with unexpected boldness. 'The second, Alessandro. The first happened years ago, when you listened to your father when he told you it was all right to go to any lengths to take revenge on someone who had hurt you or your family. Well, it's not all right! You can't use people the way you used me. It's about time you realised that.'

'I have realised it,' he said in a low voice. Then he added, to her astonishment, 'And this is the first time I've ever done it.'

Her eyes flew wide open. 'Why did you do it, Alessandro? *Why*?'

His face darkened momentarily. 'I was so angry when I discovered what had happened to Giulia. Nothing seemed more important than making Paul James pay.'

'And it didn't matter that I had to pay as well?'

'I told you, I thought you were shallow and promiscuous. The kind of girl who would see the whole thing as just one more bedroom adventure.'

'And you obviously still think I'm that kind of girl!' she retorted. 'Why else would you accuse me of taking a lover?'

He was silent for a long time. His face was set into a tense, frozen pattern, as if he were rigidly keeping control of his expression. 'I don't know what the hell to think!' he muttered at last, the words sounding as if they had been forced out of him. Then he stood up abruptly and strode out of the room, leaving most of his meal untouched.

Francine wanted to run after him, but didn't. She felt as if she were standing on shifting sand. If she took the wrong step, it could be dangerous, oh, so dangerous.

There were no apologies from Alessandro over the next few days for his accusations, but he looked oddly ill at ease. Like a man who knew he was in the wrong, but refused to admit it.

She knew that she had to tell him about the baby, but she could never quite find the courage. He had become so withdrawn, so unapproachable. At the same time, she felt a secret thrill of excitement every time she dressed in something that was a little too tight for comfort. She could hardly wait for the swell of her stomach to become obvious, so that she could believe it was really happening.

The golden glow of early autumn covered the city, the weather warm but no longer sultry. Francine explored with new enthusiasm, she seemed to be suddenly full of energy, she couldn't sit still for more than a few minutes. And she was glad to get away from the palazzo during the day, because she had deliberately begun to avoid Angelina. Alessandro's housekeeper had very sharp eyes, and Francine didn't want her to guess her secret before she had found a way to tell Alessandro.

On a particularly beautiful day, she returned from a trip to the island of San Francesco del Deserto, where she had wandered around the thirteenth-century cloister and visited the church where St Francis of Assisi was said to have stayed. Her skin glowed from the sun, her feet ached from walking, and she felt tired but relaxed and happy. Perhaps she had brought some of the peaceful atmosphere of the island home with her, she thought with a small smile, as she flopped on to one of the big, comfortable sofas in the drawing-room.

She kicked off her sandals and unclipped her hair, so that it fell in a blaze of loose curls around her shoulders. The palazzo was quiet and tranquil. Angelina had prepared the evening meal and left, but Francine didn't feel like eating just yet.

I'll wait until Alessandro comes home, she decided. And tonight, I'll tell him. Somehow, I'll find the right words.

She felt good, once she had made that decision. She felt the last of the tension slipping away, and she stretched out on the sofa, gave a small sigh of contentment, and closed her eyes.

Alessandro walked in a couple of minutes later, just as she was on the verge of falling asleep. Francine looked up at him, blinked dozily, and then gave him a sleepy smile.

'You look very relaxed,' he said a little huskily, sitting on the arm of the sofa. 'And welcoming,' he added, his eyes drifting over her and darkening several shades.

As if he couldn't help it, his hand moved towards her, and he ran just one finger lightly up the sole of her bare foot. Her toes instantly curled in response, and Francine briefly closed her eyes as a stream of sensual sensations trailed in the wake of his finger.

'That's nice,' she whispered, almost holding her breath because this was the closest she had been to him since that disastrous night of the party.

'I know a lot of other nice things to do,' Alessandro murmured, his voice sounding like pure velvet.

He lightly tickled her foot again, and she couldn't bite back a small groan of pure pleasure. Then she looked up at him. Because it was still warm, his shirt was open at the neck, and she could see the fine skin at the base of his throat; the small pulse that beat quickly in the strong column of his neck.

His hand began to explore the slender line of her ankle. Francine swallowed very hard. What was he going to do next?

She soon found out. Alessandro played gently with her toes, as if she were a child. There was certainly nothing childish about her reaction, though. And he knew it!

His eyes gleamed brightly with satisfaction. She waited tensely for him to touch her again but, with an effort, he held back. Instead, he looked down at her, his face suddenly more guarded.

'I wish that I knew the truth about you,' he said softly. He seemed almost to be speaking to himself.

'Why can't you trust your own instincts?' she said in a voice even lower than his own.

'Because they keep telling me different things. I don't know what you are, a devil or an angel.'

'I'm neither,' she said steadily. At the same time, her heart thumped with sudden happiness because she knew that *this* was the right time to tell him, while they were so unexpectedly in tune with each other. She took a very deep breath. 'But I am going to be the mother of your child,' she told him with a mixture of pride and shyness.

She searched his face anxiously for the first signs of pleasure. She was so sure that he would be pleased, a son—or daughter—to carry on the name of Zancani.

For the first few seconds, there was no reaction at all. He's in shock, she thought with a sudden grin. Well, so was I when I first realised what had happened!

Then she felt a chill suddenly roll over her because Alessandro's face was finally changing. Darkness spread across his features, giving them a frightening fierceness, and a deep glow of anger appeared in his eyes, turning them to a threatening shade of grey.

Francine felt herself involuntarily shrink back. What on earth was wrong? Didn't he want children? Had she made a terrible mistake in assuming he would be delighted at her news?

In a sudden movement, he caught hold of her wrists, and pulled her to her feet. He forced her to stand directly in front of him, and his eyes bored down into her with such fury that she immediately began to shake.

'If you're having a child, it certainly isn't mine,' he said in a totally grim voice. 'Who's the real father, Francine? *Who is it*?'

'It's you,' she choked, absolutely devastated by the accusation behind his words. 'It's you, Alessandro!'

'Liar!' His eyes burned so brightly that they almost seemed to sear her. 'I don't know whose bastard you've got in your stomach, but stop trying to pretend it's mine.'

She couldn't believe he could say such awful things to her. And he looked so furiously, uncontrollably angry that, for the very first time, she was actually afraid of him.

'I should have guessed you would do something like this,' he went on contemptuously. 'You are your father's child; you're like him in more ways than I even suspected!'

She was still so appalled and destroyed by his reaction that she found it hard to string half a dozen coherent words together. 'I'm n-not—not—like my father——' she stuttered.

Alessandro cut in ruthlessly. 'No wonder you were so eager to marry me! You probably suspected even then that you had a problem. Were you looking for someone who would give you the support—especially the financial support—that you needed? Bad luck, Francine,' he said cruelly. 'You chose the wrong husband. I don't raise other people's bastards!'

Suddenly, she was as angry as he was. 'Don't you ever call our child a bastard again,' she said fiercely.

'*Our* child?' he repeated scathingly. 'Drop the pretence, it isn't working. I've no idea whose child you're carrying—perhaps you don't either, God knows how many beds you were in before our marriage. Or after. But one thing's certain. I'll never acknowledge it, and it'll never bear the name of Zancani.'

She shook her head in bewilderment. 'Why are you behaving like this? Why can't you believe it's your child? I know that we only made love once, but that's all it takes. And neither of us were careful, not careful at all, so there's no reason why this baby shouldn't be yours.'

'It wasn't a question of carelessness on my part,' Alessandro said, his face darkening still further. 'I didn't take any precautions because they weren't necessary.'

'Not necessary?' she echoed, puzzled. 'I don't understand——'

'Then let me spell it out for you,' he said in a very tense voice. 'The crash that finished my racing career also left some internal damage. Everything works perfectly—as I proved to you on our wedding night—but there are no end results. All the pleasure in the world, but it's a sterile pleasure, Francine. I'll never have a son to carry on the name of Zancani. I'll never have any children at all.' There was a note of pure pain in his voice, now, but the expression on his face warned her not to offer sympathy, he didn't want her pity.

The shock of his announcement completely silenced her. As it slowly wore off, though, Francine felt as if she were finally beginning to understand this complex man she had married. The sophisticated lifestyle, the drive for success, the parties, the women—all of them designed to disguise a terrible inner emptiness. Even the revenge he had taken on her father took on a new meaning, it was just one more thing to occupy him, to take the place of the one thing he thought that he could never have—a family.

Except that the child she carried *was* his. But he refused to believe it. She had the terrible feeling that he was never going to believe it.

Pure despair washed over her. What on earth was she going to do? What could she possibly say to make him believe that she was telling him the truth? Or would he force her to leave the palazzo immediately, without giving her the chance to say anything more at all?

Alessandro must have guessed the thoughts running wildly through her head, because his eyes hardened.

'Don't worry,' he said in a harsh voice. 'I won't throw you out. Not straight away. But keep away from me, Francine. I don't want to talk to you. I don't even want to see you. And I want you to make arrangements for alternative accommodation as quickly as you can.'

Before she could plead with him to listen, to try and believe what she was telling him, he turned round and strode quickly out of the room. And the rigid set of his shoulders warned her not to follow him.

Until now, Francine had thought that her wedding night had been the most awful night of her life. This was an entirely new level of pain, though, and for a long while she sat just hugging herself, as if he had hurt her physically as well as emotionally. She had been afraid that he might think she was using the baby to try and keep him in this marriage against his will, but she had never, ever expected such a savage reaction.

Francine dazedly shook her head. What was she going to do *now*? She just didn't know, she didn't even seem to be able to think straight. Everything had completely crashed to pieces around her, and she had absolutely no idea how to put her life back together again.

After a long, long, sleepless night, Francine finally reached a major decision. She was *not* going to let Alessandro walk away from his child! He needed it too much.

She had to find a way of convincing him that this baby really was his. She didn't know how, but she had to try.

She showered, dressed, and went downstairs. Although it was still early, sun blazed in through the palazzo windows, making her heavy eyes ache. Francine suddenly felt as if she needed coolness and shadow, and she remembered the small courtyard at the back of the palazzo. It was shaded by a couple of trees, ferns flourished in its sunless corners, and the small fountain moistened the air. She could sit there for a while until the cool air had cleared her fevered head. Then she might be able to think of a way of approaching Alessandro.

The heavy door that opened on to the courtyard stood slightly ajar. Francine pushed it fully open, and then walked towards the old wooden seat set beneath the low, spreading branches of one of the trees. Before she could sit down, though, she realised that someone was standing motionless on the far side of the courtyard.

She licked her lips as she found herself facing her husband. 'I—I didn't know you were here,' she said unsteadily.

Alessandro advanced towards her, his shoulders rigidly set and his face under a frightening amount of control.

'I said that I didn't want to see you again,' he reminded her grimly.

'That's difficult, when we're still living under the same roof!'

'Then I suggest you leave.'

His terse words suddenly goaded her into action. Her head whipped up and her green eyes blazed straight into his.

'Do you know who's going to be the loser in all this, Alessandro? You! You could have had it all, a proper wife and a family. But you're going to throw it all away, and be left with nothing!'

He took another half-dozen steps towards her, looking so fierce that she instinctively backed away. That made him stop dead and fresh anger showed on his face.

'Why are you shrinking away from me like that?' he demanded. 'What the hell do you think I'm going to do? Hit you?'

'No,' she said at once. 'I know you wouldn't do something like that.'

'I wish I could,' he growled at her with sudden savagery. 'Perhaps it would get this whole thing out of my system if I could just beat you and throw you out!'

They stared at each other, both frightened by the violence of their emotions. And there were other, equally dangerous feelings, shimmering in the air between them. Francine was starkly aware of the magnetic physical attraction that had been there from the very beginning. And there was something else; something that went so much deeper, and perhaps was the thing that had kept them linked together in this strange marriage.

She knew that Alessandro was also vividly aware of those darker undercurrents. He muttered something furiously under his breath, and then ripped his gaze away from hers.

'Why did I ever get involved with you?' he said bitterly.

'Because you wanted revenge on my father. But it's backfired on you, hasn't it?' Francine said with far more boldness than she felt.

'It certainly has,' Alessandro agreed grimly. 'But I was willing to admit I behaved badly. I've tried to accept responsibility for my actions, and I've allowed this marriage to go on. But I won't accept another man's child!'

'This baby is yours,' Francine said a little desperately.

'Don't lie to me. I'd respect you far more, Francine—despite what you've done—if you'd just tell me the truth.'

'It *is* the truth!' But it was useless, his face was set into those stubborn lines again and she knew he was never going to accept it. Frustration welled up inside her and suddenly ran out of control, she rushed forward and gripped hold of the fine material of his shirt, ineffectively trying to shake him. 'Why do you keep trying to ruin everything?' she shouted at him, tears streaming down her face now and blurring her eyes. 'Why are you always so damned arrogant and sure that you're right all the time?'

Alessandro caught hold of her wrists, holding her at arm's length. 'Don't try that old trick!' he warned.

'What trick?'

'Trying to get close to me. Making me touch you, hold you.'

'I wasn't trying any trick!' she denied vehemently.

'Of course you were. Because you know that, when I get near to you, I can't stop myself doing *this*.'

His mouth closed over hers in a hard kiss, forcing her lips apart so that his tongue couldn't be denied access. The touch and taste of him were pure agony, Francine wanted to cry all over again with frustrated love.

'Perhaps I should just take what I want,' he said thickly, briefly raising his head. 'You are still my wife, and it would be a small compensation for what you've done.'

His hand seized her breast and the swollen tenderness turned to pleasure as he caressed her hard nipple pressing against the thin material of her dress. The muscles in his neck were rigid, as if he were forcing himself to stay away from her mouth. As she melted under his touch, though, he gave a faint groan of defeat and his lips seized hers again. At the same time, his hand slid down between her legs, and Francine almost buckled as new and intense waves of pleasure washed over her.

'You like that, don't you?' Alessandro murmured with almost savage satisfaction. 'I like it, too, so touch *me*.'

She knew that, in his own way, he was punishing her, but she still couldn't resist the invitation to touch him. Her hands frantically sought the familiar hardness of his body, she had the fantastic idea that if she could make him want her enough, then everything would miraculously be all right. Heat swirled between them as she caressed, felt the hard pulse of him against her palm, while his fingers slid right inside her, to the hottest and most secret parts of her body. She felt a small glow of triumph, he was hers, he belonged to her! Then, from somewhere, Alessandro found a vestige of self-control, he pulled back, broke the contact between them with cruel abruptness.

'You're a very clever girl,' he said thickly. 'You know all my weaknesses. Know how to exploit them.'

'If I were that clever, I wouldn't have got pregnant,' Francine said in a voice that was suddenly dull. She knew that she had lost him. Her moment of triumph had lasted for only a few seconds.

'That was certainly a bad mistake,' Alessandro agreed tautly.

She looked at him with all the sadness of the world in her eyes. She knew now that she was never going to be able to put things right between them. 'I think that it's best if I leave,' she said in a completely defeated voice. 'We can't go on like this.' She certainly couldn't. It was killing her.

'Where will you go?' He seemed to ask the question very reluctantly, as if he hated admitting that he had any kind of concern for her.

'Back to England, I suppose. I've still got a flat there. And I can find a job,' she said with a forced show of bravado.

'Employers don't fall over themselves to take on pregnant women,' he said abruptly. 'You'll need financial help——'

'No, I *don't*,' she said with one last surge of fierceness. 'I don't want anything from you, Alessandro.' Except his love, which he would never give her. 'Just let me go.'

She turned and almost ran out of the courtyard. Fresh tears were streaming down her face and she didn't want him to see them.

She went straight up to her room and began to pull her clothes out of the cupboards and drawers. It suddenly seemed imperative to get away from here *right now*. Francine knew that she ought to make plans, get in touch with people who could help, at least phone the airport and book a ticket. She didn't do any of those things, though. If she couldn't get a ticket, then she would just wait at the airport until there was a cancellation!

She knew that if she stopped to think about the future, then she would probably get very frightened indeed. No husband, no job, no parents at hand to help her. Resolutely, she closed her mind to all the terrifying problems that lay ahead of her, and continued to pile up her clothes on the bed.

'Where are my suitcases?' she muttered to herself, looking around a little frantically. She didn't know, they must have been stored away somewhere, and she didn't want to waste time looking for them. She just wanted to run away from the Palazzo Zancani and never come back.

She remembered that there had been a couple of suitcases stacked on the top of the wardrobe in Giulia's room. She didn't think that Alessandro's sister would mind if she borrowed them. She rushed blindly along to the room, in search of them.

The cases were exactly where she remembered seeing them. She hauled them down, and was about to run back to her own room when the door to the en suite bathroom suddenly opened and a girl walked through it, and into the bedroom.

She was extraordinarily pretty, with a cloud of dark hair and huge grey eyes. She had obviously just showered because she was wearing a thin, damp bathrobe, and her bare feet were leaving small, wet patches on the carpet.

'Hello,' she said in surprise. 'Who are you? And why are you stealing my suitcases?' Then her face suddenly cleared. 'I know, you must be Francine. You're my brother's new wife.'

Francine looked at her in astonishment. 'You're—you're Giulia?'

The girl grinned. 'That's right. I arrived this morning on a surprise visit. Alessandro doesn't even know I'm here.'

Giulia's English was as faultless as Alessandro's, and she even had a faint trace of an American accent, obviously picked up during her extended stay in that country. Then Francine remembered what had happened to Giulia in America, and she slowly put down the cases.

'I don't know quite what to say to you,' she said in some embarrassment.

'Why ever not?' asked Giulia in surprise.

'Because—well, because of who I am,' Francine said uncomfortably.'

'Alessandro's wife?' Giulia said in a faintly puzzled voice. 'But I don't mind about that. I know there's been just the two of us since our parents died, but I'm not at all possessive about my brother. I always knew that he would get married one day—although he's managed to put it off for a very long time,' she finished with a grin.

'No, it isn't anything to do with that.' Francine could feel the colour mounting in her face. 'It's because of my father,' she said very awkwardly. 'You must know that I'm Paul James's daughter. I'm surprised that you even want to talk to me. I mean, I know what happened. I know what he did to you. Alessandro told me,' she finished with a rush, wishing that she had never started this conversation because Giulia probably hated talking about it, she probably didn't even want to *think* about it.

But Alessandro's sister looked amazingly unconcerned. She walked over to the dressing-table, picked up a brush, and drew it in slow, almost sensual strokes through her dark hair.

'Don't worry about it,' she said carelessly. 'Your father didn't do anything dreadful.'

'Of course he did! I know all about the party and—and what happened afterwards,' she said, feeling dreadfully embarrassed all over again.

Giulia gave her a conspiratorial smile. 'Look, I want us to be friends, and we can't be if you believe that your father did something awful to me. Can I trust you?'

'Well—yes,' she said, wondering what was coming next.

'You'll promise *never* to tell any of this to Alessandro?'

'Any of what?'

'The truth.' Giulia gave a small sigh. 'I adore my brother, but he always sees me as his little sister, someone he's got to protect. The truth is that I've been grown up for a very long time. And I like older men. Your father wasn't the first and he almost certainly won't be the last.'

'What are you saying?' Francine asked slowly.

Giulia giggled mischievously. 'He didn't seduce me. *I* seduced *him*. We had a lovely time together—nothing serious, of course, I don't plan to settle down with anyone for years yet. Only Alessandro suddenly walked in——' Giulia's eyes rolled extravagantly '—and I knew I was in serious trouble. I didn't know what to do, so I threw myself straight into his arms and played the part of the ravished virgin. I sobbed, I pretended I'd had far too much to drink, I even had hysterics. And it worked!' Her eyes gleamed with fresh amusement. 'It was very naughty, of course, but it did get me out of trouble. And I wasn't too worried about your father; I knew he had the kind of reputation that could easily take a few more dents.'

Francine was stunned into total silence. Everything that had happened to her—*everything*—had been because this girl had told a string of lies to protect her own reputation?

Alessandro had never needed to avenge the seduction of his sister, because Giulia had jumped very willingly into Paul James's bed. All that Francine's father had been guilty of was giving in to the temptation to have a brief affair with a beautiful girl who was far too young for him.

For a few moments, Francine found herself fiercely hating Alessandro's lovely, amoral young sister. Did she have any idea how much unhappiness she had caused? Or even care? Then she reminded herself that Giulia couldn't have had an easy life. Her father had obviously been a stern and difficult man, and for the past few years she hadn't had any parents at all. Francine knew from personal experience how hard it was to get through the traumatic teenage years without any proper help or guidance from parents; how easy it was to make the wrong decisions, or go down the wrong path.

All the same, she knew it would be a long time before she could completely forgive Giulia for what she had done.

'By the way, you never told me why you wanted my suitcases,' Giulia reminded her. She was spraying expensive perfume on to her body now, and only half paying attention to Francine.

'I'm going away,' Francine said quietly.

'With Alessandro? How on earth did you entice him away from his business affairs? He's a workaholic!'

'I'm going on my own.'

That made Giulia's perfectly shaped eyebrows shoot up. 'Goodness, it's a bit early in the marriage to be taking separate holidays, isn't it? Of course, I know that Alessandro's rather difficult to live with,' she chattered on. 'He has such dark moods at times, and he's got a quite fearsome temper! Look, I'm afraid I'm going to need those suitcases myself,' she said, changing the subject with lightning speed. 'Sorry, but they *are* mine.'

'Aren't you staying at the palazzo?' asked Francine in surprise.

'No, this is just a flying visit to collect some clothes. I whizzed in this morning because I was sure that Alessandro would be at work. I told you, he's always worked ferociously hard, and I was sure even a new marriage wouldn't change that. Be an angel, and don't tell him I was here.'

'You don't want to see your brother?'

'I'm on my way to the South of France for a couple of weeks,' Giulia explained. Without the slightest trace of embarrassment, she tossed the bathrobe aside, slid into a thin silk shift dress, and wriggled her feet into high heeled sandals. 'I met this film producer in America, and we're—well, taking a little holiday together. He thinks that I'm just right for a major part in his new film, but he wants to get to know me better before finally offering me the role. If Alessandro finds out, though, he'll hit the roof. I want him to think I'm still in America, being chaperoned by Aunt Isabella.'

'And where does Aunt Isabella think you are?' asked Francine a little tightly.

'On a flying visit to Italy, to see Alessandro,' Giulia said cheerfully.

'One day, you're going to get caught out by all these lies,' Francine warned.

'Of course I am. But until then, I intend to have a lot of fun. *And* advance my career.' She was tossing clothes haphazardly into the cases now, designer dresses being shoved in carelessly along with shoes, lace trimmed undies, skimpy swimsuits and exotic beachwear. Then she glanced round. 'That's everything, I think. Right, I'm off. Remember, not a word to Alessandro. Don't even tell him that I was here.'

But Francine had had more than enough of Giulia's little games, she wanted no part of them. 'And what if I do tell him?' she said rebelliously.

'Oh, I wouldn't do that,' she warned. 'He's going to hate whoever brings him that particular piece of news. And he's going to be so very angry that no one in their right mind would want to be within a hundred miles of him! Alessandro is *dangerous* when he loses his temper completely.'

With that casual threat delivered, Giulia waltzed out of the room, leaving Francine standing there feeling quite stunned by this first encounter with her sister-in-law.

It was a long time before she finally moved. She had almost forgotten that she, herself, had been on the point of walking out. Still shattered by all these latest revelations, she walked slowly towards the door. Just as she reached it, though, Alessandro appeared in the doorway, every inch of him dark and forbidding.

Before she could even catch her breath, he had seized hold of her arm.

'Get back inside,' he said tensely, and when he had forced her back into the room, he slammed the door shut behind him.

'What do you want?' she somehow managed to get out, recoiling from the pure fury on his face.

'Want?' he said fiercely, his eyes blazing brilliantly with the force of his emotions. 'Just for once, I would like the truth. And you're going to give it to me, Francine!'

CHAPTER NINE

'WELL?' Alessandro demanded. 'Did you intend even to tell me that my own sister came here this morning, to the palazzo?'

'You saw her?' Francine said with a small gulp.

'And heard her. I was passing her room, I recognised her voice—and yours.'

Her heart almost stopped beating. 'How—how much did you hear?'

'All of it!'

'Then you know——'

'That my sister has behaved like a little tramp?' he cut in harshly. 'That she's lied, done things that would have broken her mother's heart if she'd still been alive? Yes, I know,' Alessandro said with utter grimness.

Francine felt a sudden ache inside her, because she knew how much Alessandro was hurting under all that anger. 'You said that *you* were wild when you were young,' she reminded him. 'Why should Giulia be any different?'

He didn't even seem to hear her. 'I tried so hard with her,' he said bitterly. 'She was only ten when our parents died, she had all the difficult adolescent years still ahead of her. I tried to guide without being too strict, to advise without seeming to lecture. Obviously, I failed completely!'

Francine laid her hand on his arm. 'No, you didn't. She's bright, as well as beautiful. She'll come through this all right. You've just got to stand back and let her make her own mistakes for a while.'

'But to behave the way she has——'

'Don't blame yourself. Even if your parents hadn't died, this would probably still have happened. Giulia's got a lot of spirit.' She gave a small, wry smile. 'She's very much a Zancani.'

'My father would have stopped it,' Alessandro said tautly. 'He would have beaten her for such behaviour, and gone on beating her until he was quite certain she'd never do anything like it ever again. Perhaps I should do the same.'

'You would never raise your hand to her. Or to anyone,' Francine said with complete certainty. 'And you're right, because that isn't the answer. She needs love, not abuse. Perhaps that's what she's looking for, only she's looking in all the wrong places.'

Alessandro moved restlessly around his sister's bedroom before finally coming to a halt by the window.

'None of the reasons for our marriage were ever valid, were they?' he said abruptly.

'Not on your side,' she said more quietly. Her reasons for marrying him were perfectly valid. She had loved him. She *still* loved him, in spite of everything that had happened. It was amazing—and a little terrifying—that nothing he ever did could destroy the feelings she had for him.

'I wanted revenge for a seduction that never took place,' Alessandro said, his tone very still tense. 'I was too angry to listen to the voice inside my own head, telling me that it was wrong!'

'At least you've learned something from all this,' Francine said steadily. 'You won't make a mistake like that ever again.'

'But in the meantime, what do I do about *this* mistake?'

She flinched at that blunt question. She was still a 'mistake', their marriage was something that he had never wanted, it had all been part of his complex scheme to hurt her father in every way possible.

'You don't have to do anything about it at all,' she said, fighting to keep her voice from betraying too much. 'As soon as I've packed my things, I'm leaving. You won't have to see me ever again.'

His head came up sharply. 'But things have changed.'

'No, they haven't,' she retorted, suddenly finding a new strength and determination from somewhere. 'You don't want me and you don't want my baby, so we're both getting out of your life!'

'You're not going anywhere,' Alessandro told her bluntly. 'Not yet.'

Francine knew that she had to get away, though, or this situation was going to shred her nerves to pieces. She stood up very straight, even though her legs were shaking madly. 'Try and stop me!'

'Like it or not, I'm still your husband. I'm responsible for you.'

'I don't need anyone to be responsible for me. I'm an adult, I can run my own life.'

'You've no job, no income, no permanent home,' Alessandro reminded her darkly. 'Your father lives in a Hollywood dreamworld where he still tries to behave like a young heart-throb, and your mother wanders around the world, rarely bothering to come home or even keep in touch. And now, you're pregnant. I'd say that you definitely need help from someone, Francine.'

'But not from you,' she insisted fiercely. She knew that it would really destroy her, having to live with the knowledge that he was only helping her because he felt sorry for her.

His face became shadowed. 'Are you refusing my help because I called your child a bastard? I apologise unreservedly; I should never have used such a word. No child deserves a label like that.' He paused, then added with some difficulty, 'And there are a great many other things that I probably need to apologise for.'

'Such as our wedding night?' Francine reminded him, and this time she just couldn't keep a note of bitterness out of her voice.

'Yes,' he agreed with grim reluctance, as if the memory of his unforgivable behaviour were something that he would very much like to erase for ever.

'Well, I'm sorry,' she said, choking a little over the words, 'but an apology isn't quite enough, Alessandro.'

'What do you want me to do?' he demanded, his eyes suddenly blazing sheer green. 'Go down on my knees? Beg for forgiveness?'

Quite suddenly, she had the extraordinary feeling that he would do just that, if she insisted on it. She didn't want to see him totally humiliated, though. All she really wanted right now was to get away from here before he caused her any more pain.

'I just want to *go*,' she said a little desperately.

'And if I won't let you?'

'You can't stop me!'

'I think I can,' said Alessandro. His gaze fixed on her with unswerving intensity. 'I think I can make you an offer that you would be a fool to refuse.'

Francine found herself gently shivering under the sheer force of his gaze. 'What—what kind of offer?' she whispered.

'I'll adopt your baby after it's born,' he said steadily. 'I'll give it my name, a secure home and a future.'

She stared at him in sheer disbelief. 'How can you do that?' she cried, shaking her head so wildly that it hurt. '*How can you adopt something that's already yours*?'

Blindly, she pushed past him, she couldn't bear to look at him, or even be near him, any longer. She wrenched open the door, hurtled towards the stairs, and was so wrapped up in the aching pain inside her head and heart that she didn't even hear her own scream as she lost her footing, and went tumbling down and down and down.

Francine slowly became aware of the soft murmur of concerned voices. She didn't want to hear them, though, she kept her eyes closed and blotted them out. She thought that she slept for a while. Or perhaps she was unconscious. When she next woke up, it was because of physical discomfort. Small aches and pains in her arms and shoulders, and one of her legs. But not in her stomach, she realised with a sudden flood of relief. Thank God, not her stomach.

But she needed to make sure. She forced her heavy eyes open and tried to focus.

'My baby?' she croaked.

It was Alessandro's voice that answered her. 'Your baby is fine. He—or she—is obviously as tough as you are.'

She bit her lip. She didn't think that she was tough. Right now, she just wanted to bawl her eyes out.

'You bounced down the stairs like a rubber ball,' Alessandro went on, his voice sounding very strained. 'The doctor says you're covered with bruises, but that's all. Nothing broken, no internal damage.'

For the first time, Francine forced herself to look at him. She was surprised to see that his face was pale and drawn. She gave a choked giggle that somehow turned into a half sob. 'You look worse than I do!'

'That's probably because I thought you'd killed yourself. Don't ever do anything like that again,' he said tautly.

'I won't,' she promised. She moved her stiff shoulders, and gave a small groan. 'For one thing, it hurts too much.'

'Everyone seems to be getting hurt in this. And I don't mean just physically.'

'I know,' she said in a subdued voice. 'But I tried to do something about it. I tried to leave.'

'And only succeeded in nearly breaking your neck!' The colour drained from his face even further as he relived the moment when she had taken that terrifying fall.

'I'm still going to go,' she said with sudden stubbornness. 'As soon as I'm well enough.'

'We'll discuss that later. Right now, you've got to lie still and rest.'

'I'm feeling better already,' she insisted.

'The doctor left orders that you were to stay in bed for two days.'

'I'm getting up in the morning,' Francine said with determination.

'Two days,' Alessandro repeated, and something in his tone warned her that he intended to be obeyed.

In the end, she did stay in bed for the next forty-eight hours. But not because Alessandro had ordered it, she told herself, her eyes flashing. It was because she didn't want to do anything that might put her baby at risk.

She was fussed over and cosseted by Angelina until she began to feel quite stifled. And during the short periods she was left on her own, when she was meant to be sleeping, she lay and worried about the future. Francine knew that she had to make plans. In a few months she would have a baby to support. The thought both excited and terrified her, as well as making her immensely sad, because she knew that she was going to have to raise a child who would never be acknowledged by his—or her—father.

But, for now, she had to be practical. She still had her flat—it had been a twenty-first birthday present from her father—but very little money and no job. She was sure that her parents would help, but she hated the idea of taking money from anyone. And she certainly wouldn't accept a single penny from Alessandro.

On the third morning after her fall, she got up early, showered and dressed. She felt a little wobbly on her legs, but the bruises were much less painful. During the night, she had made a decision. She would leave the palazzo this morning, and fly back to London. If she had to make a new life for herself, then it had better be straight away. Why stay on here and just make it more painful for everyone?

She went downstairs, to phone the airport. She had to book herself a ticket. When she went into the drawing-room, though, Alessandro was already there.

The sight of him jolted every nerve in her body and made even her skin feel painfully raw. God, how was she going to walk away? Face the thought of never seeing him again?

As she stood there, just staring at him, a faint flush of colour showed on his own face.

'How are you?' he asked, his manner oddly formal.

'I'm fine,' she said in a fractured voice.

'You don't sound it. Or look it. Sit down,' he ordered. 'There are some things we need to talk about.'

'I don't want to sit,' she said tensely. 'I want to leave.' And right now, because she had the awful feeling that she was going to burst into tears if she had to face him much longer.

'Francine, sit down and listen!' he said abruptly. 'This is very hard for me to say, and I can't do it if you're going to run out on me before I've finished.'

Startled by his brittle tone of voice, she quickly seated herself in the nearest chair. Alessandro moved around restlessly, though, he seemed to be finding it impossible to stay still. Finally, he swung back to face her.

'After the doctor had been to examine you, after your fall, I had a private discussion with him,' he said, speaking very quickly. 'I had some very personal questions to ask him.'

'What kind of questions?' Francine asked in a low voice.

'You were so insistent that the baby you're expecting is mine. I knew that it couldn't be—but I needed to be sure. I asked him to rerun the tests that were done after my crash on the race track.'

Francine realised she was holding her breath. 'Did he do the tests?'

'Yes.' Alessandro's face darkened. 'He warned me that I should expect the same results. The tests would show I was still incapable of fathering a child.'

She hardly dared to ask the next question. 'And—did they?'

His features revealed nothing, his brow, his mouth were almost rigid, as if he were keeping every single one of his emotions very tightly in check. 'It seems that, against all the odds, there's been some slight improvement,' he said at last, in a voice that didn't sound at all like his own. 'The doctors can't account for it, it shouldn't have happened—but it has. The baby you're carrying could be mine.'

'Of course it's yours,' she said with sudden fierceness. 'What do I have to do to make you believe it completely? Wait until it's born, so you can see how much it *looks* like you? Because it will, I know it will. Or are you going to insist on blood tests, just to be absolutely sure?'

'No, no blood tests,' Alessandro said, his voice still very odd. 'I think—if you'll let me—that I'd like to begin to be a father right now.'

Francine sat absolutely motionless. This was what she had wanted from the very first moment she had suspected her pregnancy. She ought to be laughing, dancing, deliriously happy. Instead, she felt strangely numb. Slowly, she began to realise that it wasn't enough. She couldn't live in an empty marriage, where she and Alessandro only stayed together for the sake of their child. Her baby needed a father and a mother, she knew that, but there were also things that *she* needed to make her life complete and give it some kind of meaning. She couldn't be a proper mother if she were only half a person.

'I think it's too late,' she said at last in a very flat voice. 'It won't work.'

The first signs of shock showed on his face. He obviously hadn't expected any kind of rejections. 'What do you mean, it won't work? I can give you—and the child—everything you'll ever need!'

'I can't live in a marriage that doesn't mean anything. All the money and luxury in the world——' she gestured around her, at the opulent interior of the palazzo '—it can't compensate for a loveless relationship.'

'Are you saying that you don't love me?' Alessandro demanded tightly.

Her green eyes were shadowed with pure sadness. 'I don't think that you even care if I love you or not. I'm just not important to you in any way, especially now that you don't have any reason to want revenge on my father.'

'How can you say that you're not important?' he said incredulously. 'You're the mother of my child!'

'But I want to be more than that!' she said with sudden passion. 'I want to be loved for myself, not just because I'm going to give you the heir that you thought you'd never have.'

Alessandro was silent for a very long time. He seemed to be fighting something inside himself, conflicting emotions chased across his shadowed face. At last, his eyes fixed on her face again, suddenly very clear and bright, as if he had reached a major decision.

'And what if I said that I was already in love with you when I married you?' he said very quietly.

She shook her head tiredly. 'I wouldn't believe you. You couldn't treat someone you loved the way that you treated me.'

'I could, if I despised myself for falling for someone I thought was shallow and promiscuous. The daughter of a man I loathed and hated so much that I wanted to kill him,' Alessandro said in a low tone.

But Francine had been through too much, she just couldn't accept what he was saying.

'You want me to stay with you because of the baby,' she said in a drained voice. 'You'd say anything, do anything, to try and stop me leaving. Even tell lies about loving me.'

Alessandro strode over, pulled her out of the chair, and then gripped her hands so tightly that she could feel the imprint of every one of his hard fingers.

'I wouldn't lie about something as important as this! Look at me, Francine,' he ordered in a jagged voice, as she tried to drag her eyes away from his brilliant grey-green gaze. 'You think these last few weeks have been hell for you? Well, they've been a nightmare for me too! I've wanted you so much that I've nearly gone out of my mind. I haven't been able to sleep, eat or work. When you told me about the baby, I thought that I really would go quite mad. I was so sure you had a lover, it nearly killed me to think of him kissing you, touching you, giving you his child.' A deep shudder ran through his body, as if he couldn't bear thinking about it even now. 'But I *still* loved you,' he went on, the words pouring out of him with an intensity that he couldn't seem to control, 'still couldn't stop wanting you. I despised myself for being so weak, I told myself that I'd throw you out, never see you again, force myself to forget you, but I couldn't do it. And, in the end, I realised that I'd do anything, absolutely anything at all, to keep you. I'd even accept another man's child and raise it as my own. Nothing was important, except making you stay with me.'

His impassioned confession shocked her so much that she couldn't say a single word.

'You don't believe me, do you?' Alessandro said a little desperately. 'You think it's just a trick to stop you walking out.'

'I—I don't know,' she managed to get out in a totally dazed voice.

'What do I have to do to convince you? Tell me!' he demanded. Then he ran his fingers into his black hair. 'Hell, there's no way that I *can* convince you,' he muttered. 'You're always going to believe that I want you to stay because of the baby. That love's got nothing to do with it.'

His eyes were bleak with despair, she had never seen him look like that before. So tormented, so willing to let her see all the emotions that he usually kept under iron control, but which were now tearing him apart.

'I just want what's best for you,' he went on, dragging in an unsteady breath. 'God knows, I don't want to cause you any more unhappiness.' His mouth twisted in new pain. 'Perhaps the only way I can really prove I love you is by setting you free. And I'll do it,' he promised, 'if that's what you decide that you want. It'll nearly kill me, but I'll let you make a new life for yourself, away from me.'

Francine was still reeling from the torrent of words he had thrown at her. He *loved* her? He really did love her? A new, cautious hope began to glow inside her. She warned herself against it, but she just couldn't seem to stop it growing.

'I don't want a new life,' she said unsteadily. 'But I don't want the old one either, it was too painful. I want what I've got right now, but I want it to include you, Alessandro. I need to know that you're telling me the truth, though. I really couldn't stand it if this was just one more deception.'

Alessandro could see the doubts clearly written on her face, and his own eyes took on a tortured glow.

'You can't trust me, can you? And I don't blame you. I can't make you believe I'm telling the truth this time.' He suddenly looked deathly tired and defeated. 'Perhaps you should just forget about me. Walk away now, while I'm still willing to let you go. If you don't have any feelings for me, that would be kinder. Except that I don't really deserve kindness, do I? I don't know what kind of punishment would be suitable for the way I behaved—except, perhaps, never to see you again.'

She couldn't let him go on tormenting himself any longer. 'I don't want to punish you,' she said softly. 'And I don't want to walk away. I'm probably the biggest idiot in the world, Alessandro, but all I want is to stay here with you, forever.'

His eyes briefly glittered. Then they went dull again. 'It's the baby, isn't it?' he said flatly. 'You're staying because you've decided that your child needs a father.'

'Our child,' she corrected him, with the first faint hint of a smile. 'And I'm staying because of *you*. I loved you when I married you, and I'm probably completely crazy, but I still love you. And if I can't stop loving you after everything that's happened these last few weeks, then I don't think I'm ever going to stop!'

But he obviously didn't believe her. Wouldn't let himself believe her.

'Look, both of us need convincing of a few things,' she said. 'Perhaps a kiss would help.'

Slowly, as if almost frightened to touch her, Alessandro bent his head and let his lips slowly rest against hers. The temptation to go further soon became irresistible, though, and the kiss swiftly became harder, more intense, and they were both breathing very unsteadily by the time they finally broke apart again.

'Do you think I was faking that?' Francine asked shakily.

'No,' he admitted huskily.

'Would I kiss you like that if I hated you?'

'No,' he said again, his eyes darkening.

'*Now* do you believe that I love you? That I'm not going to leave?'

'I think that I'll have to,' Alessandro said, his voice and body slowly relaxing as he finally began to accept that he wasn't going to lose his wife, or child. 'But I'd like you to go on convincing me,' he added, his voice a dark velvet invitation.

Francine was aching to do just that. 'All day and all night,' she whispered, her mouth already hungry for the hard warmth of his lips again.

This time, his hands also moved against her, sliding eagerly against her breasts before suddenly becoming still again. 'The baby——' he said uncertainly.

'If it can survive a fall down the stairs, then it can certainly survive a few kisses.'

'I might not be able to stop at a few kisses,' he warned.

'I hope you can't. I don't really feel properly married,' Francine told him, her eyes dancing mischievously. 'I'd like a *proper* honeymoon this time.'

Alessandro's hands moved restlessly, and she felt a fresh wave of heat break from his body. 'I think that I can make you feel *extremely* married,' he promised throatily. His words made her heart beat wildly under his palm, and she was aware of the quick, answering surge of desire in his own body. 'But I don't think I can wait until we get to the bedroom,' he warned softly. 'In fact, I think we'll be lucky to make it as far as that large, comfortable sofa behind you!'

But they somehow managed it. The warm autumn sunshine poured through the window on to their bodies as they quickly pulled off each other's clothes. Alessandro ran his fingers with intense curiosity over the slight changes in her body, his lips traced a path over the tiny swell of her stomach, and he played gently, very, very gently, with her tender breasts.

And Francine, in turn, adored being able to touch him freely in return. She loved his smooth, heated skin, the hard muscles underneath, the knowledge that the desires of that powerful body were being kept strictly in check because he was absolutely determined not to hurt her in any way.

'I must have been mad to have fought against this for so long,' he murmured in a muffled voice, his face briefly buried in the bright tangle of her hair. 'Why did I put us both through such misery?'

'Because you thought that you had a good reason for hating me. And because you had too much stubborn male pride!' she added, her eyes smiling at him.

Alessandro eased his body closer to hers, his breathing quickening as, hard and ready, he still held back, deliciously prolonging the moment that they both longed for.

'Tell me, *cara*,' he said with fresh urgency. 'Tell me *exactly* how you feel about me.'

'I love you,' she said simply. What a wonderful relief it was to be able to say those words! 'I've loved you since that night we first met. Nothing you did to me or said to me ever changed that.'

'I don't deserve it,' he told her huskily. 'But I intend to spend the rest of my life making sure that you're loved very thoroughly in return.'

His mouth returned to hers, to seal his promise with a kiss that made her heart beat even more fast and furiously. His hands lightly caressed, eased her legs apart, caused quick flutters of excitement and then a slowly mounting sensation of a deep and highly sensual pleasure. Francine touched him in return, her fingers lingered lovingly over his hot, hard body, she thought he was the most beautiful man she had ever seen and he was *hers*.

She heard the breath rasp in his throat as he fought for control.

'No more,' he warned raggedly. 'I want to be careful——'

And he was, feathering light kisses across her breasts before softly, softly licking the small hard tips into total submission. Taking his weight on his arms so that his powerful body didn't crush her. And when he finally slid inside her, it was with exquisite gentleness. Francine was totally captivated by this new and sensitive side of him. And the care he took didn't detract from the overwhelming pleasure which built and built, carrying both of them to the very edge of the precipice. In fact, it only added to it, the slow strokes of his body prolonging the delicious sensations to the point where neither of them could bear them any longer. She clung on to him fiercely, and let him carry her over the last threshold, to a world that was saturated with love and pleasure and happiness.

Francine let out a loud yell that was partly pain and partly triumph as her baby at last slid from her straining body.

Beside her, Alessandro gripped her hand very tightly and looked so white that she was afraid he might do the traditional thing and pass out! Then he stared down at the small, squirming bundle, and the colour flooded back into his face.

'It's a boy!' he said in wonderment. 'And he's perfect. Just like you!'

Their son filled his lungs and then let out a cry that was almost as loud as his mother's had been, as he had been born. Francine gave a huge smile of exhausted satisfaction. Then she raised her head so that she could see more clearly the baby resting against her stomach, his dark hair still damp, his small face screwed up and turning bright red as he began to bawl again.

'He's very ugly,' she said drowsily and lovingly. 'But he'll soon be as handsome as his father.'

The midwife bustled around busily, but Francine lay back and enjoyed the first rest she had had in nearly twelve hours. She had done all the hard work; all she had to do now was to enjoy her new baby.

'I think I'd like a girl next time,' she said, gently stroking her son's soft head.

Alessandro looked at her in amazement. 'You want to do this all over again? Go through all that pain?'

'It did hurt a *lot*,' she admitted. 'But it was only for a few hours. And it was worth it,' she said, looking at their son tenderly.

'Just don't become pregnant again too soon,' he said a little huskily. 'I'd like you to myself for a while.'

'I'd like that, too,' Francine said softly. The last few weeks had been frustrating for both of them, as she had got too big for them to be able to make love properly. She, too, was already looking forward to being able to curl up close to him again.

She gave a small sigh of contentment. She had never thought her marriage could be so perfect. There had been a few small problems, of course. Alessandro's relationship with her father was very cool, and probably always would be. He had got on surprisingly well with her mother, though, when she had finally returned from her trip to India and Nepal, and come to visit her daughter and new son-in-law. And Giulia had learned the hard way that taking a holiday with a film producer didn't guarantee a movie career. She had returned to America and was now taking acting lessons with a qualified teacher. She had been very subdued when she had learned about the trouble she had caused, and was now making a determined effort to grow up and put the wild phase of her life behind her.

Francine looked up at her husband and he smiled back at her, a smile which was full of love and need and passion. Then she fell gently asleep, with her baby beside her and her husband still holding very tightly on to her hand, as if he would never let her go.

THREE TIMES A LOVE STORY

A special collection of three individual love stories from one of the world's best-loved romance authors. This beautiful volume offers a unique chance for new fans to sample some of Janet Dailey's earlier works and for long-time fans to collect an edition to treasure.

WORLDWIDE

AVAILABLE NOW PRICED £4.99

Available from WH Smith, John Menzies, Volume One, Forbuoys, Martins, Woolworths, Tesco, Asda, Safeway and other paperback stockists.
Also available from Worldwide Reader Service, FREEPOST, PO Box 236, Croydon, Surrey CR9 9EL. (UK Postage & Packing free)

HEARTS OF FIRE

What will happen to Gemma now that Nathan seems determined to end their marriage?

And can Celeste spend the rest of her life taking revenge on Byron and building up her empire? Can she continue to deny all those long-buried feelings?

All will be revealed in...

SCANDALS & SECRETS
by Miranda Lee

Book 5 in the compelling HEARTS OF FIRE saga.

Available from July 1994 Priced: £2.50

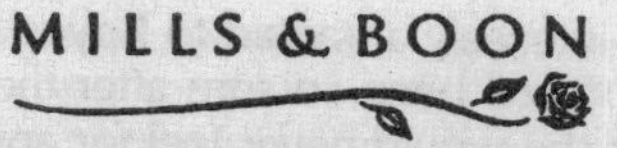

Available from WH Smith, John Menzies, Volume One, Forbuoys, Martins, Woolworths, Tesco, Asda, Safeway and other paperback stockists. Also available from Mills & Boon Reader Service, FREEPOST, PO Box 236, Croydon, Surrey CR9 9EL (UK Postage & Packing free).